The Invitation

Baron Alexander

Wilderwick Press

Forest Row, UK

Dedicated to Joe

CONTENTS

The Road Not Taken

While on the frosty road less travelled, I came across a lone figure. My choices made, I made another and stopped to offer him a lift.

"Where you heading?" I asked. I was driving to forget and looking for company.

"North," he said.

"Hop in."

He did. He put his bag in the back seat and joined me in the front.

"Is that all you got?" I said, looking at his bag.

"Yep."

He was late middle aged, bearded, and wearing a heavy coat. There wasn't much more I could see from where I was seated. All I knew was he would be dead if someone didn't pick him up soon.

"Waiting long?" I asked.

"Yeah. Not too many people pick up hitchhikers these days. Thanks." He shrugged and tried to smile. The cold must have frozen most of his face but I understood the gesture.

"I'll let you warm up before I start talking at you too much," I said. He didn't respond. "I've got a thermos of coffee in the back if you want something to drink. There's probably a sandwich and some chocolate if you'd like."

"You sure?"

"I wouldn't offer if I wasn't. Help yourself."

He did. He poured a coffee for me, black, and one for himself. A few minutes later, he must have started thawing out, as he took off his coat and put it in the back seat. He then unbuttoned a heavy flannel jacket, which he left on, and rubbed his hands on the sweater underneath to warm himself. I expected him to have an odour but was pleasantly surprised. I probably smelled worse than him.

"Do you smoke?" I asked.

"When I have the chance. What do you have?"

"Just tobacco," I said, realizing how it could've been misconstrued.

"Works for me. I only smoke tobacco."

"Sorry, I didn't mean anything by it. I was just trying to be friendly."

"I've got cigars on me if you like but you may not be too keen on smelling up your new car."

"It's a rental."

That got him interested. "Where you heading?" he asked.

"North sounds good to me. I've been driving since Dallas. Need a change of scenery. I looked on a map and saw Churchill and thought northern Canada was as good a destination as any. You know, polar bears and all that."

He smiled. "Running or rough patch?"

"One hell of a rough patch. Just need to clear my head."

"You know you can't drive to Churchill?"

"Uh, yeah. I figured that out when I passed Winnipeg and picked up a map. Who would've thought?"

He was silent for a bit. "I'm heading to Churchill too. My plan was to grab the train from Thompson. If you still want to go, that's really your only option unless you want to fly. But you don't seem like you're in any great hurry."

That made me smile. "Sounds like a plan."

"You driving through the night?"

"Was planning to but I think Thompson's only around seven more hours. That should get us in just before midnight."

"Assuming the weather co-operates," he added.

It didn't. Three hours out of Winnipeg and two hours after I picked up my new travelling companion, the wind picked up and the snow on the fields started blowing across the road. At first it was a pleasant scene, something out of a National Geographic landscape. The grand expanse of white with a setting sun created an orange hue as we followed the black tarmac. There was no snow falling but the stuff on the ground was being driven onto the road, clawing back at civilisation. Snow fingers thudded against the tires as we drove. I slowed down, turned the lights on, and watched the first snowflakes fall. I never even thought about the weather. Who the hell thinks about the weather? That's what good cars are for. The reality is that if you can't see the road, you can't drive.

By the time this dawned on me, panic set in. There weren't many towns along this route. I kept my eyes peeled and gripped the wheel.

"Don't white knuckle it," he said.

"Huh?"

"Relax your hands on the wheel. Slow down and let the car drive. We'll be okay."

"Easy for you to say. I've never seen snow like this, let alone drive in it."

"Do you want me to drive?"

I hesitated. I didn't know this guy from Adam, but he sure seemed like a survivor. Not many would try hitchhiking in this. I decided that was worth more than my spotty driving skills. Besides, my nerves were shot and all the romance of clearing my head and driving north had taken a backseat.

"Okay," he said. "Take your foot off the gas, but don't hit the brake. The last thing we want is to start spinning at this speed."

That just made me more nervous. I hadn't considered the risk of spinning out. I allowed the car to drift to a halt. When we were stationary, my hands were cemented to the wheel. I managed to pry one hand off and put the car into park. I pried off the other and sat back in my seat, sweating. I actually welcomed the blast of cold when I opened the door to switch seats.

"You okay?" he said as we settled into our new positions.

"Yeah. Thanks. I owe you one."

"No. I owe you for picking me up. Sit back, have some of your chocolate, and I'll get you to the next town. I think its Grand Rapids. It's not glamorous but I'm pretty sure they'll have some sort of hotel."

I sank into my chair and watched the snow in the headlights. The sun was down and it felt like we were driving at warp speed, stars racing towards us. Blackness all around. The warmth of the heating and the exhaustion of non-stop driving sent me to sleep quickly.

When I awoke, we were stationary again. The snow was still falling, heavier than before. There was a glow of lights off a white building next to us. He parked us right in front of the hotel entrance and left the engine running as he went inside. When he returned, he was smiling and held up a set of keys.

"They only had one room but it has two beds. I told them okay. I don't think we have too many options. The restaurant is still open for another hour or so. That should get us enough time to unpack and grab a bite before everything shuts down."

"Thanks," I said. "What do I owe you?"

"Nothing. My treat."

I thought it odd him hitchhiking but having enough money to pay for a room. At the time, I didn't care too much. I just wanted out of the wintery hellscape and for the sun to rise again.

I grabbed my suitcase and emptied the car of anything that might explode when frozen and joined him in the small, dingy room.

∞

Calling the establishment a hotel was being kind; it was a motor inn. It was of wood construction, built some seven decades ago, with a steep roof and aluminium front doors. But it was shelter from the cold and I was thankful. The beds were lumpy and the covers had a hint of an odour that fell somewhere between urine and vomit despite clearly being heavily bleached and washed. I didn't care. It was warm and the heaters were sufficient to keep the cold outside. We ate some semblance of food in the restaurant and had a few drinks in the motel's bar. The people were friendly and couldn't have been more helpful with directions, stories, and sympathy at our plight. Under different circumstances, I could see myself liking the place.

The next morning, I awoke to the glow of the radio's red clock. It was almost eight and still dark outside. My travelling companion was snoring slightly, but it hadn't woken me. I had a shower and shaved and readied myself for the rest of the journey to Thompson.

"How's the weather looking today?" I asked the waitress as she poured my first coffee.

"Look out the window, hon."

"Is that normal?" I asked.

"Normal enough. Looks like a big one. I don't think anyone's going anywhere for a few days."

"I'm sorry?"

"You haven't heard? Biggest storm of the season blowing in. You were lucky to get here when you did last night. We're expecting up to fourteen inches but the wind'll continue for days. It'll take a good day or so after it stops before the roads open up."

I put my coffee down. I wasn't in any great hurry, but I wasn't expecting this.

"Have you decided what you want yet?"

"I'll have the special. Sunny side up with brown toast, please." I figured there was no sense in starving if I was going to be stuck here. I just wasn't sure what I was going to do for the next few days. At that point, the hitchhiker joined me.

"Hear the news?" He grabbed a chair and sat across from me.

"Yup. Not too great."

"Oh well, can't complain. We're in a decent place with hot food and all the amenities. Could be a lot worse."

"Not much," I grumbled.

"Believe me, this is heaven. And from what I can surmise from you and your situation, this may be just what you needed."

I tried to smile. He was just too damn optimistic. "Not sure if you're qualified to say that," I said.

"You'd be surprised. Let's grab some grub and I'll tell you a story that'll make you happy to be alive."

We finished breakfast and, having nowhere else to go, we positioned ourselves in the motel bar. It was next to the breakfast room and had a large television on the far wall with the only comfortable armchairs in the whole place. It was early and we figured we'd be un-disturbed there. The waitress saw us move spots and offered a carafe of coffee.

I'd never really met any celebrities. Not really. The closest I came was walking into a small diner one even-ing where I met an aging comic I idolised in my youth. I was star struck and, trying to be nonchalant, said hello and offered my hand. He shook it and cracked an inside joke about one of his movies. I laughed politely and he went on his way. His handshake wasn't extraordinary in any way. It was a hand. Not a particularly firm hand-shake either. The whole experience was less than I expected. The hitchhiker, on the other hand, continued to surprise me.

As he started talking, I realised I was in the presence of a person who had truly lived a life, one who knew powerful people and had equally powerful enemies. *You can judge the measure of a man by his enemies,* I'd once heard. This is the story he told me.

Jack

The table was set, the champagne and wine were chilled, and Jack felt the little box in his pocket. Tonight he would ask Sarah the question he knew he'd ask her from the moment he met her.

He looked around and there was nothing to do but wait for Sarah to arrive. He started to tidy up the kitchen. A knife was lying halfway along the cutting board and, when he reached for it, he suddenly jerked back his hand. He was shocked at the thought that flashed through his mind. He could see himself grabbing the knife and plunging it into himself. He never had a thought like that before and it scared him deeply. He decided to get out of the kitchen and away from that knife.

As he turned to leave, he looked down and saw the knife plunged just below his sternum into his stomach.

∞

The next thing Jack remembered was Joe next to him, sitting in the big chair next to the hospital bed. Every boy needs a father or mentor to help him become a man. For Jack, this was Joe. He had always been there, with his white hair and prospector-like stubble. His clothes were clean and relatively tidy, though he didn't iron his shirts very often. Jack's parents knew him from way back and were happy for their son to be spending so much time with him.

Jack's parents were government employees. They had job security, but their lives were uneventful. They lived in a small town of a few thousand people and were over an hour's drive from the city. It was safe and quiet, but Jack never really fit in when growing up. He tried music, but that didn't take. He tried sports and was pretty good. He had a few friends and they would pass the time cycling around town, throwing a ball or playing some basketball, or would veg out with movies and video games.

Joe lived two doors down. When his parents went out of town for conferences or business trips, Joe would keep an eye out for him. Today was one of those days and Jack was glad he was there. He found out later that Joe did the time from his home to the hospital where Jack was now laid up in just under 45 minutes. The nurses had to come in and get Joe to remove his car from the hospital entrance—but only after he had seen Jack's doctor and received confirmation that everything was okay.

"Wha--?" Jack muttered. His lips and brain were numb.

"Just take it easy, son," Joe said. He rose and stood next to him, holding his hand. "You've had an accident. Everything's okay. You're in the hospital. Sarah is here. She's just run down to get some coffee."

Jack looked at Joe. Worry was writ large on his face, the lines and creases more pronounced. His scraggly white hair was unbrushed and his watery eyes were full of concern.

"Sarah found you. If she hadn't come when she did, you would have bled out." Joe swallowed and took a moment. "You scared us, Jack."

"Mom? Dad?"

"They're on their way from the airport. Shouldn't be long now."

"Sarah?"

"She's fine. Covered in blood and shaken, but fine. She's a good egg, that one." Joe smiled. "It was an accident, wasn't it?" His eyes met Jack's and bore deep as he waited for a reply.

"I don't know what happened," Jack said slowly. "I was making dinner and everything was finished and I saw the knife and the next thing I was here." It was the truth. He didn't remember touching the knife. It must have been an accident. It wasn't until later, alone with his thoughts, that he started to piece things together.

Just then the attending doctor walked in. He looked young to Joe. *Which is the first sign of old age*, he thought to himself. "Hi doctor. Any news?" Joe said.

"Everything is looking fine. Surgery was uneventful and the stitches should heal up in good time." The doctor closed the file he was reading. "I don't know the details of what happened, but you were very lucky. There's no major damage to any of the organs and you should make a full recovery in in around 6 weeks."

"When can I leave and do I need to come back?" Jack asked.

"I'd like you to stay in for at least three more nights. Nothing strenuous for a few weeks after that. The internal stitches will dissolve so you don't need to worry about that. The external stitches can be dealt with in 7-10 days. Just monitor things and watch out for infection."

"Do I need to come back here?"

"Here or any walk-in will be sufficient. When you check out, book in a time to come back and we'll take things from there. You'll be fine Jack."

"Thank-you, sir." Jack's relief was palpable. Or maybe that was just his body reacting to the pain killers. "Good to know there's no permanent damage."

The doctor shook Jack's hand and left.

Joe put his hand on Jack's shoulder and, now that his main worry was over, changed direction of the conversation. "Planning a big night?" A twinkle returned to Joe's eye.

Jack squirmed a bit. He didn't want to jinx his proposal but he told Joe anyway. "I was planning to ask Sarah to marry me," Jack said, "but I think I ruined the moment." He managed a little laugh. It hurt.

Suddenly two arms grabbed him, lifting him from his pillows. Sarah held him tight and was crying. Her hair covered Jack and he could smell her perfume and warmth. Her tears wet his cheeks and she kissed him deeply.

"Yes," she said.

"What?" Jack asked.

"Yes, I'll marry you!" She covered him with kisses until he was forced to make some noise, as the pain from his belly was still stronger than the drugs.

Joe shook Jack's hand and kissed Sarah's cheek. "Congratulations. I was starting to think this day would never happen." He smiled.

"Me neither," said Sarah. She was beaming. Her white teeth, reddened cheeks, and tears were the picture of bliss.

It was some time later, almost an hour, before Jack's parents arrived. Joe had left to get some food for everyone and Sarah was sitting next to her fiancé.

"Jack!" His mother came through the door and smothered him with kisses and a tender hug, careful to not disturb his wound too much. "We've been battling traffic to get here. Anyway, that doesn't matter. I've heard from Joe the operation went well and you're okay." She paused for a breath and then, "How are you?" Her words came out faster than they should have. She wanted to hear from her son directly that everything was okay.

"I'm okay Mom. I don't know what happened. I'm just glad I didn't kill myself." He felt awkward. Nervous.

"Jack, don't even kid about something like that." His father entered the room. There was a smell of smoke on them both.

"You guys start smoking or something?"

His mother laughed. "No, but it goes to show you how sensitive a non-smoker's nose can be. We got laid up with some colleagues who smoked like chimneys."

"How're you feeling, son? You scared the hell out of both me and your Mom." Jack's father had tears in his eyes. "Are you sure everything's okay?"

"Better than okay." Jack always felt better when his parents were next to him, regardless of the recent events. "Mom, Dad, I have a bit of news." He reached for Sarah's hand. "Sarah and I are getting married!"

Jack's mother's hands raised slightly and she took on a delirious look on her face. "Oh, that's beyond wonderful news. I always wanted a daughter," Jack's mother was crying tears of joy now. "Come here Sarah." She wrapped her arms around her. Sarah started crying again.

"Congratulations son," his father said. "I'm proud of you."

Despite the knife wound, the frantic phone calls and the hospital environment, spirits couldn't have been higher. It was a good day.

∞

Carey met Jack just over three weeks after the knife incident. Carey liked what she saw and struck up a conversation.

"You look pleased with yourself," she said. "Having an exceptional day are we?"

"Are you talking to me?" he asked, his eyebrows slightly raised. Ever since his hospital stay, his studies had begun slipping. He had spent almost an entire week in the hospital instead of the three days. He was getting around fine now but it was still slow going. He wanted to get back into a routine and this meant more time on campus, in the library, and eating whatever this café had to offer.

"Yeah. Sorry. You look so happy and most people here are so miserable. I just thought…" She paused and wiped her palm against her pant leg. "Hi, I'm Carey."

"Hi, Jack. Nice to meet you." He felt a little awkward. Carey wore some airy yoga-type clothes that showed, with little to no imagination, that she was fit. She looked Icelandic with her brown hair and light blue eyes. He snapped into reality and looked straight at her. She didn't wear much make-up, only a lip liner and a little something around the eyes. They positively sparkled.

"Uh, what was the question?" He was feeling a little foolish now.

"You look happy," Carey smiled. She knew this response. So far, so good.

"You bet. Happiest time of my life. I asked my girlfriend to marry me a few weeks back and she said yes. It still hasn't sunk in. It feels like she just said 'yes' today." He smiled again.

"Congratulations! When's the big day?" Carey said the words but realized that this was a lost cause. He did seem nice, though. *At least he didn't lie about it,* she thought to herself.

"Haven't set a date yet. Probably in June after we graduate."

"What're you studying?" On campus the question was automatic, like dogs sniffing each other's butts.

"Commerce. She's studying architecture." Jack was proud of his degree and even more so of Sarah. She had real talent. "And you?" Jack almost forget to ask.

"Law. I graduated last year and I've secured a position at a pretty good firm, but it still means a lot of library time on campus. The firm has a decent library and the law society is great, but I still like coming here. It'll probably change once my lease is up on my apartment. I'll move closer to the firm. Easier all around."

Carey was easy to talk to and easy to look at. Jack made the appropriate excuses and carried on to his class. Carey's eyes followed him. He piqued her interest and it wasn't just his height and athletic build. There was a sadness in him, despite the smiles. She liked him and decided to befriend him. *Maybe it's possible for guys and gals to be just friends*, she thought.

She ordered a black coffee with milk to go. She also had a smile to go with the spring in her step.

Over the next three weeks, Carey found herself accidently bumping into Jack quite often. But there were others as well—girls who had no business being in that particular café. Those whose only purpose seemed to be hunting for their next boyfriend. *Bitches*, Carey found herself thinking on one occasion when, trying to bump into Jack, found herself amongst three female students all who just happened to need some coffee at that particular café. And who all felt themselves compelled to ask idiotic questions of Jack. All standing an inch in front of him. All trying to look casual but their motives were paper thin. But then she smiled to herself and thought, *bring it on.*

∞

Life should be great, Jack thought to himself as he settled into reading the newspaper. *If I could only solve this problem...* The apartment only had one sofa, bought used, and one armchair. He sat in the chair and perched his coffee at his elbow, with his feet up on the coffee table. He rarely had time for such luxuries what with his studies—and he meant to make the most of it. He reached for his coffee and enjoyed the peace. It gave him time to think. It was getting close to six weeks since his trip to the hospital and he was looking forward to the rest of his life with Sarah.

When the door closed, Jack got up to greet his fiancée. His smile disappeared as she hit him squarely in the face.

"You bastard!"

"What the--? What the hell, Sarah?!"

"Why, Jack? Why now? Why her?"

"Why her what? What the hell are you talking about?"

"I know Jack. I've seen the pictures. Don't lie to me on this. If you've ever loved me, don't lie to me on this." She was incandescent with rage. Her face was flushed and her hair sparkled with sweat.

"Calm down! I really don't know what you're talking about."

Sarah was in the kitchen fumbling around with a glass. She poured some wine into it and gulped it down.

"I received an envelope of pictures and mobile phone records. It was you and that girl, the one who keeps *accidently* bumping into you. Even last week she just *happened* to get a coffee at the same place and time we meet after class. There were pictures of her naked. With you. You and her in some room. Ring any bells?"

"What girl are you talking about? Carey? Zara? Kelly? Mrs. T?"

"Don't play dumb, Jack, it doesn't suit you. The Asian bitch bimbo from fine arts who wears those black tights and sweat-shirt tops. Athletic. Sexy. At least now I know why." Sarah slammed the envelope on the table and fumed. She waited for Jack to reach for it.

He did. When he looked at the pictures, he began to laugh.

"You think this is funny, you sonofabitch?" Sarah picked up the magazine closest to her and threw it at him. He ducked.

"I've seen her before. We both have. But this isn't me. I mean, it looks like me but it isn't. I don't even know this woman's name."

"You don't need to know her name to fuck. So what was she? An urge? Am I so ugly and boring you need to find some slut to fuck? What's wrong with you?" Sarah's head continued to shake.

"I'm saying this isn't me. These photos have been tampered with."

"And the phone records? You can't tamper with those. It shows texts and phone calls from your number to hers on a daily basis, sometimes over ten times a day."

"I don't know what to say other than it's all lies. I never called or texted her, not once."

"So you're saying it's all a conspiracy? I may be a small town girl, Jack, but I'm not a fool."

"Sarah, there's nothing going on between this woman and me. You'll have to just trust me on this. I can't tell you anything more."

"Can't tell me anything more? Who the hell do you think you are? I accuse you of cheating on me and you tell me to trust you that you haven't? Even when I have evidence?"

"I know it sounds insane. But yes, I can't tell you any more other than that it's all lies. If I say any more, they may come after you as well. This little manoeuvre by them was just to show me what they're capable of."

"*They*? Are you on drugs?"

"I love you, Sarah."

"And right now I hate you. I can't be here. I'm taking the car. I'm going to my parents'." She grabbed some clothes, textbooks, and an apple and stomped out of the apartment. "I can't believe I said yes to you. You're one sick bastard." He heard the door slam.

Jack stood there looking at the closed door. There was no sense in running after her or making a scene. He was innocent and he knew exactly who was doing this: Clog.

∞

Detective Warren Clog of the CIA came to see Jack around two months prior, just a week or so before the knife incident. He said he had proof that Jack's parents were deep cover spies imbedded in America. Their cover allowed them to be away for extended periods of time on 'conferences' when really they were making contacts or exchanging information with the enemy.

Clog rambled on about how the two were US citizens but were traitors and deserved to hang. Their role was to spy for the highest bidder, and worked as mercenaries, doing jobs for anyone who would pay. They were the conduit for secrets that ended up in Russia, China, and Israel.

He went on to explain that they were merely cogs in a much larger network of espionage, which was the CIA's real target. What concerned Clog, the CIA, and Homeland Security was that they had remained undetected for twenty-five years, despite the resources available to the government to monitor, eavesdrop, and disrupt operations like this. The discovery of Jack's parents and their activities was an accident.

Clog's job was to keep the status quo.

"Then what do you want from me, Detective? That's assuming everything you told me is true—and I'm not sure I believe any of it. I would have noticed if my parents were spies."

"You're a good boy, from everything I've been able to find out about you," he said. "You have nothing to worry about from me."

"Then why are you here?" Jack repeated.

"I have a proposal for you. I don't want you to answer me right now. I want you to take a couple of days. I'll be back and we can discuss it further."

"What do you propose?" Jack said. He didn't like this. In movies or spy novels, nothing good happened from situations like this.

Detective Clog had a simple proposal: spy on his parents, don't tell anyone about the arrangement, and live happily ever after. If his cover was blown, Clog would see to it that Jack would receive the full punishment possible—but outside the courts. Clog vowed to destroy Jack's life on a personal and professional level if he told his parents or anyone else of the operation.

"Do you know how rare it is for us to find an asset like you?" Clog asked. "The money, time, and personnel employed to get us where we are today has been enormous. What I am asking of you is your patriotic duty as a citizen of this great nation. If you aren't with us, I have no option but to consider you an enemy of the state."

Jack was in mental and emotional overload. He was being asked to betray his parents. Or had they betrayed him—and America? What about Sarah? Secrets are the seeds of divorce and unhappiness. He didn't like keeping secrets from people he loved and trusted. It wasn't in his nature.

"So you come out of nowhere and demand that I betray my family without any proof other than your word and my patriotic sense of duty. You then threaten me with unspecified harm if I don't comply."

"You're a smart boy," Clog said. "You got it in one. Don't take too long." He left his card on the table and closed the door as he let himself out of Jack's apartment.

Jack sat down, shaking. He felt violated. He was just a student and this was something out of his wildest nightmares.

∞

The weekend after Clog gave him the ultimatum, Jack decided to go home to visit his parents. Perhaps he could see them through fresh eyes. As it happened, they were away at a conference in San Francisco.

He stopped by Joe's instead. The smell of warm oil and cut wood always relaxed him. Joe was fiddling with something on his work bench and his face lit up when Jack walked in.

"How 'ya doing, Jack? Studies okay? How's Sarah?"

"Good, good, and great." Jack couldn't help but feel better. Joe had this effect on him.

Jack watched Joe work for a while, but the old man sensed that he had come for a reason.

"What's up? Everything okay?"

"Yeah. No. I need some advice."

Joe put his tools down, turned off the magnifying glass light, and pushed its extending arm out of the way. He swivelled to look at Joe.

"Is Sarah pregnant?" Joe asked.

Jack chuckled and smiled. "No, no. That wouldn't be a problem for me. I can't wait to have children with her, but she wants to pursue her career first." Jack smiled at the thought. He hadn't even thought about kids for a long time.

"Money?"

"No. Money is okay, thanks."

"So you're not pregnant, no money troubles. Is it another woman?"

"Joe! I'm not playing twenty questions. And no, there's no other woman." Jack smiled despite himself. "Why would you presume it's another woman? Maybe Sarah found another man!"

It was Joe's turn to chuckle. "Easy. Sarah loves you and she's not stupid. You, on the other hand, are a guy. And we're all stupid when it comes to that."

"Maybe," Jack said.

"Seriously," Joe said, "what's eating you?"

"It's hard to explain and part of the problem is that I'm not supposed to talk about it."

"Sounds ominous. Can you tell me anything?"

"I had someone tell me something that has serious consequences. If I tell, they will hurt me, Sarah, and the family."

Joe was silent.

"I know I should stand up to bullies but this isn't an ordinary situation. This bully can't be beaten, and it is above the law."

"No one is above the law," Joe said. "It may seem like it, but they aren't. Abuse of power is something us common folk frown upon. Is there any way to shine light on this bully?"

"No. If I shine light or talk or do anything, they'll hurt us."

"Have you been gambling? Is this the mob we're talking about?" Joe became angry and sat up a bit taller.

"No, worse. Government."

Joe was silent again. "Does this have anything to do with me?" he asked.

This time it was Jack who was startled. "What? No." He frowned. "Why?"

"No reason. I'm just trying to get my head around your problem, that's all."

Then Jack did something he knew we would regret. He told Joe everything.

∞

Shortly after his talk with Joe, he had the knife incident, became engaged, met Carey, and was now being was accused of having an affair. Bloody Old Joe. He must have said something to someone. As Jack understood it, he had two choices: Talk to his parents or talk to Clog. Was there a third way?

Did I stab myself and not remember? Or was there someone there who stabbed me? Is that even possible? His mind raced over recent events and tried to focus on the turning points. The stabbing, the photos, Sarah, Joe. His parents. Clog.

He knew what he had to do. Whether he could pull it off was another matter.

Chapter Three

Sins of the Father

"Why did you do it? You could've killed me. I thought I was going nuts until I figured it out. A knife? I thought I was a valuable asset. And Sarah, why sabotage my relationship? Wasn't the knife enough?"

"You needed reminding of our deal," Clog said.

"We didn't have a deal. You gave an ultimatum. I didn't say anything to anyone."

"Ah, the lies. Why do you lie to me, Jack?"

Jack was still. So Joe did say something. "Who said I said anything?"

"We have ears all over the neighbourhood. You didn't think that just because he was an old guy we wouldn't find out?" Detective Clog pulled out a pack of cigarettes and flicked his wrist expertly to pop one out. He put the pack to his lips and, when he withdrew his hand, the cigarette was in his mouth. In a fluid motion, he lit it, put the packing in his inside pocket, and inhaled.

"I didn't say anything. I was just asking a friend for some advice."

"Don't bother denying it. We have you on tape. You spilled your guts to this guy even though you knew—or should have known—who you were dealing with. Your underbelly and your relationship with Sarah was just a warning shot. I wanted to meet with you before we did anything else."

Jack wasn't sure what to say. It meant his parents' home was under surveillance and possibly even his apartment. It also meant Joe's place was bugged. It seemed like overkill. The good news was that Joe wasn't the problem. Jack was his own worst enemy for shooting his mouth off.

"I'll help you if you provide me with a full pardon in advance and some legally binding paperwork confirming everything you're doing is within the rule of law. I also want comfort in the form of some pardon for my parents if I'm able to turn them to become agents exclusively for the US government." Jack was surprised and impressed at what seemed to come out on its own. "I may be able to get them to provide full testimony if I can assure them of a full pardon."

Jack was finding the pressure of betraying his parents as painful as the knife and fight he had with Sarah combined. He knew he needed to play hardball with Clog on this point.

Joe was inhaling his cigarette and enjoying the nicotine hit. He closed his eyes, took a last drag, crushed the butt in the ashtray, and looked directly at Jack. "We don't negotiate with terrorists or traitors." He got up and made for the door. Just before closing it behind him, he turned and said, "You have twenty-four hours to make up your mind."

∞

23 years earlier

"It's not fair," Denise cried. James reached over and held her hand. He was silent but his eyes were filling up.

"I'm sorry to be the one to tell you this," Dr. Cook said. "But as you know, this is now the fourth session of IVF and it just isn't taking. We could try again but I am starting to think it isn't going to happen. I am deeply sorry."

"Is there anything we can do?" James asked. It was a plea on behalf of his wife's pain more than his own.

The doctor looked at the two broken adults in front of him. He had seen it countless times. The feeling of inadequacy, failure, and loss of meaning in life was overwhelming for some. "There is a possibility of you having children, but not with James' sperm. Denise's eggs seem okay. I don't want to provide false hope, but you are looking for a miracle and that may be your best bet."

"A sperm donor?" Denise felt herself recoiling. She wanted James' baby. Not some stranger's. It wouldn't feel right. It wouldn't feel like their baby. She wanted a little life that would grow and develop into a beautiful man or woman, guided by herself and her husband. To be part of and be better than both of them.

"I'm okay with that," James said. He gripped Denise's hand firmly and looked straight at Cook. He felt her head snap towards him. "I know what this means to Denise and I will always be the dad if not the father."

Denise leaned in and kissed him. "I love you," she said.

Dr. Cook watched the familiar scene unfold and waited for the right moment. "Okay, let me know when you'd like to proceed. There are numerous sperm banks available for your selection…"

"No," interrupted Denise. "I'd prefer to know the donor. Is that allowed? Can we search and find our own sperm? I know that sounds creepy but I'm confident the right person is out there. Also, I'd like to know more about the personality we're getting into. What do you think, James?"

"Uh huh." James was trying to put on a brave face for his wife.

"No problem," said Cook. "Our office is always open to you both. Call when you have found your specimen." He smiled and got up from his chair, shook their hands, and left the appointment room. It was normal to allow patients time to compose themselves before they left.

As it happened, they did find the right person. All they needed was to figure out how to approach him. He lived only a few doors down on their street. He was a good looking man who allowed himself to appear rougher than he was. It all clicked into place when Denise heard some gossip about a bastard son of Einstein living in their town. It seemed so unlikely that she laughed along with the hairdresser and thought nothing more of it. But then she started thinking about this man in her midst who had the DNA of greatness in him. James laughed at the suggestion.

Her body froze with excitement and fear when Denise saw him and forced herself to approach him. He was shopping in the vegetable section and carefully examining some aubergines. As he chose two and put them in his basket, he found himself face to face with Denise.

"Hi," she said. "I don't think we've met. I'm Denise and my husband James is just down aisle four. We're neighbours. Well, on the same street." She was babbling and tried to force her mouth to shut.

"Nice to meet you, ma'am," he said.

"We've only moved to town a year ago and our work keeps us so busy we don't have much extra time to socialise. I feel terrible that we haven't met and talked before this."

"I've seen you both around. I remember you because you hold hands when you walk. You also leave for work around 7 a.m. in a blue Ford." He noticed her looking at him. "It's a small town and I like to watch people," he said by way of explanation. "It's better than TV."

"Okay, now I feel even guiltier," she said.

At this point James joined them and introduced himself. They shook hands.

"Say, do you want to join us for dinner tonight? We're making a roast with all the trimmings…"

He hesitated but said, "Sure. I'd love to. When do you want me to drop by?"

"Arrive at 6:30 for drinks and we'll eat around seven. Is that too late for you?"

"No, it's perfect. Can I bring anything?"

"Absolutely not, Mr. Steinberger."

"Please, call me Joe."

∞

Jack took the bus back to his home town, since Sarah still had his car. He didn't want to call his parents but he needed to talk to them. In person.

He walked from the bus stop to his childhood home. Everything looked smaller now when he visited. When he was growing up as a child, the local mall looked massive, the greasy spoon was cool, and he could see himself growing old in this town. Now, it looked empty, lonely, and sad. It lacked the energy of the city, and he no longer wanted to spend his life there.

As he approached his home, he saw the plain Chevy pickup in the drive and the second car, a VW, parked on the street. Mom and Dad were both home. Good. He walked confidently up to the front door, opened it (it was never locked when they were home), and walked in. It felt like home. There was a corridor that ran alongside the garage and the house that was full of jackets, boots, and a chest freezer. All the seasons' clothes were either hanging on the wall for immediate use or within easy reach behind a door on the wall units. Jack could smell the rubber of the winter boots and the slightly mouldy bits of carpet that got wet from the snow and left for years.

He opened the inner door, which led to the area in the house where everyone would take off their boots, shoes, or sandals and put on slippers or just walk in their socks. Shoes were never worn in the house. There was a little toilet and sink there as well. It was well used. Jack remembered flushing live mice down the toilet after he and his father couldn't face killing the ones they captured in their humane mousetrap. The mouse was alive and just needed to be set free or disposed of. It was cowardly, but they just slid open the side of the trap and allowed the mouse to fall into the toilet. They laughed at it swimming desperately against the swirl of the flushing water. In retrospect, Jack felt monstrous and disgusted at himself. Perhaps he was maturing or evolving. Or just becoming more civilised.

He could hear that the TV was on. They would be in the basement, probably eating popcorn. He went downstairs and put his finger to his lips when they saw him. Surprisingly, they didn't seem surprised. They were quiet. If Jack was more perceptive, he would have seen a slight trembling on his mother. They left the TV on and followed Jack upstairs, put on their shoes, and went outside. Jack waited until they were at least a block away before he started.

"Sorry Mom, Dad, but I wanted to make sure they weren't listening." His mouth felt like it had cotton in it. He felt conscious of every sound he made.

"What's going on, Jack?" His dad was looking at him in a new light. He could see something was wrong.

"Let him speak, James," his mom said.

"I have to be brief and you need to swear to me that whatever I say now will not be repeated unless I bring it up." Jack had a tremor in his voice. Defiant and demanding.

James and Denise looked at each other and then at their son. They nodded.

"I was visited by some CIA asshole who is threatening to ruin my life, Sarah's life, and hang you both. He has already shown me that he's capable of carrying out his threats."

James instinctively moved forward to touch Jack's shoulder and look at him from side to side, up and down. "Did they hit you? What did they do?"

"You remember the knife incident?" Jack looked directly at them. "No accident."

Both James and Denise recoiled. Denise held her hand to her mouth and James' face hardened. They took each other's hands and reached out to Jack.

"Why didn't you say anything?" James said. His voice was hoarse.

"Why didn't you tell me anything?" Jack replied. His was angry.

"James," Denise interrupted. "Jack, tell us. What else did they do to you?" She was trying to ascertain facts despite the desire to protect her son. The training was kicking in.

"Nothing yet. But this guy told me you two are some kind of spies who are selling government secrets. I couldn't believe it. I tried to see you the week before the knife incident but you were out. I mentioned this to Joe and the next thing I knew, I found myself in the hospital. Just when I thought everything had calmed down and I had recovered from the surgery, Sarah was given doctored pictures to show me with another woman, along with phone records. And that was just the beginning. They want me to spy on you. They won't do a deal with me or you. They have given me until tomorrow to give them a final answer."

Denise put her arm around him. "I am not going to deny it. I don't think we have the time for that. All I can tell you is that we also had no choice. We did what we thought was best at the time." She wanted Jack to know they loved him. *But how will we survive as a family?* she thought to herself. *This changes everything.*

"And we did our best to leave you out of it," James continued. "We couldn't have been more careful."

"This is weird on so many levels," Jack said. "But I don't think we have a lot of time. You must have contingency plans. What are you supposed to do in these circumstances?" Jack felt like the adult, taking control of the situation. His parents seemed dazed by the news.

James and Denise looked down. They didn't speak immediately.

"Mom? Dad?"

"You don't want to know."

"I need to know. I'm part of this now." He felt hurt to have been left out of this secret his entire life. Now that he was in, he wanted to be part of the decision making process.

"We are to kill ourselves or anyone who has knowledge of this."

The words were spoken. Jack thought he had received enough shocks to his system already, but this was at a whole new level. He couldn't speak or react. It was as though he had been shot by them right there and then. The adrenaline started to cause him to shake, making his voice wobble when he talked.

"But we can't do that," James said.

"No," Denise said. "We could never do that."

"Thanks, I guess," Jack said. "But that must leave us some more palatable options?"

"Let's think on this. We'll go home and have some food. Let's assume every room and device is bugged. We can go for ice cream after dinner. That will allow those who are listening to realise we're out for a walk. Your mom and I will talk during dinner about your school, work, and life. We'll have to leave our phones, watches, pens, and anything else that may be bugged. Your mom and I are good at this. We'll figure out a plan and we'll discuss it over ice cream at 3rd Ave and 1st later. Now, let's get back before they realise we aren't watching TV and start getting suspicious. You grab something at the diner and meet us then. You don't want them knowing we're talking before you give them your decision."

Denise hugged her son a little too long. James gave him a kiss on the neck and bear hugged him before they left him. It was the most intense emotional roller-coaster Jack had ever lived through.

∞

7:45 p.m. and Jack was walking to stay warm. It didn't make sense to have ice cream in this weather. He had grabbed some chicken and fries at the local greasy spoon, complete with a coke and a smile. There was something about small town life that appealed to him.

But walking in circles and waiting, cloak and dagger style, wasn't so fun.

7:57 p.m. and there was no-one in sight. Jack started to get nervous, but reminded himself that this is what his parents did. They would show up, have a plan, and everything would be fine.

8:05 p.m. and Jack was crestfallen. He wasn't important enough for them to fight for.

8:15 p.m. and Jack was mad. He wasn't the guilty party. Why were they making him wait?

8:36 p.m. and Jack was scared. Maybe things weren't okay. Maybe the CIA guys had already visited his parents.

8.:45 p.m. and Jack decided to return home, but circuitously. When he got there, the lights were on. The vehicles were there. Everything looked normal. He tried the front door. Locked this time. He used his key to get in. He opened the inner door. Everything looked the same. The TV was on but he couldn't smell any food. He went into the basement. No one was there. He went upstairs. No one was there.

They fled. He was alone. An abandoned child, torn between family past and family future. Torn asunder by the deception of the spies who were his parents.

Chapter Four

A New Direction

Is this how long forever lasts? Jack sat on the floor and stared at the ring. It was on the coffee table on top of a note. He hadn't read it. He feared the worst.

Instead he grabbed the bottle of scotch he reserved for these occasions and poured his first glass. It took three glasses before he reached for the paper. The contents were as he feared. His love was lost, his life was shattered. He had lost his north, his way. His solution was to drink until it stopped hurting.

The boot in the ribs didn't wake him immediately. He heard muffled sounds and then the words, "watch out, he'll rupture. He'll bleed out and die and be useless to us." The water on the face helped, but it was being physically dragged from the floor and force-walked that woke him up. It was Detective Clog. At this moment, Jack's primary goal was to focus on standing up, listening to the voices around him, and trying not to get killed.

"Have some coffee, Jack," Clog said. "Sorry about the missus." He nodded towards the ring and note. "I know it's none of my business, but I've seen this before. High school sweethearts get married and everything is great, but one bad argument can end the whole thing. Trust me, you are lucky to escape without too much damage."

Jack wasn't sure if he was dreaming or if he misunderstood. "Ah don need yor friggin advish," Jack managed. His slur was bad but the message came across.

"Okay then, I'll get down to business." Clog sat down and poured himself a drink. He made a face but still drank it. "Yesterday we had a heart-to-heart. I think we understood each other. You were given until today to give me an answer."

"Goh fug yourshelv."

"Come on, Jack. I know you're hurting, but be smart. This is a big decision. You have a great future ahead of you. Or it can end now. What's it going to be?"

Jack drank the coffee and grabbed a loaf of unsliced bread. He tore off a big piece and ate the soft bit and left the crust. He never liked the crust. He just needed something in his stomach.

"Gif me a minnud."

"You don't have a minute, but I'll let you sober up a bit. Have some more coffee. Do you smoke? No? Mind if I do?" He didn't wait for permission, just lit up and blew the smoke in Jack's face.

"Okay."

"Okay, what?"

"Okay, ahl do id."

"Do what?"

"I'll shpie on my parentsh. Jusht led me aloan rite now. I need schleep."

"I'm not usually this generous and easy going, Jack, but I'll cut you some slack because of Sarah. I'll come by tomorrow and we'll talk."

Yeah, you do that, asshole. I'll spy—like hell! I'll cut off my manhood before I rat them out to you. Jack's thoughts were clear, just speaking them was tough.

When Clog and his goons left, Jack's thoughts tumbled inside of his sobering mind, partly awake, partly asleep.

What's love that's lost so soon? Maybe Clog was right. How could she turn on me so completely? What about the truth? What about second chances? Was she so cold, so heartless, that she couldn't see past the lies?

But I loved her. Love her. Always will. I'll wait for her. I'll prove to her that I'm innocent and she'll come back to me.

Who am I kidding? Her mother, her friends, those pictures will remind her of why she should never come back. Hell, I never ran after her. I never chased her begging forgiveness. I never said sorry (even if I wasn't guilty, a sorry would've gone a long way). Maybe it's me that doesn't want the marriage.

∞

The next day started slowly for Jack. He didn't suffer from hangovers but he had consumed a lot of alcohol and his body needed to process it. A long hot shower, clean clothes and a lot of coffee helped put him back on his feet. He knew Clog was coming back and he was ready for him.

"Sorry about yesterday. It rarely happens," Jack said.

"Understood." Clog was all business. "Going forward, we'll not be meeting like this. I'll give you an encryption program which will ensure our correspondence is secure. You'll be able to send videos, pictures, and text. Have you ever used sites like these?"

Jack nodded. Clog wasn't a pleasant guy at the best of times. The information was coming at him a little too fast. He had to concentrate to keep up.

"Good. Here's the address. I suggest you memorise the site and any passwords. Assume surveillance at all times on you and your parents. Your job will be to get us the info we don't already have."

"I'll do what I can. I don't see them that often now I'm in the city at uni."

"Be that as it may, find something. We'll be watching you and remember one thing: this is a long term relationship. There is no end date. Consider this your marriage vows. 'Till death do us part."

What was there to say? Clog disappeared behind the door and Jack was alone.

∞

He reasoned there was no harm and no betrayal because his parents had skipped town. His mind was still functioning at less than optimal levels and his thoughts were staccato'd. They were probably protecting him by not taking him along. Besides, who knows what their future would hold. He still couldn't get his head around the fact that his parents were spies. It was sort of cool and bat shit crazy at the same time.

What he didn't understand was why he hadn't even cried. He must still be in shock. Autopilot mode, one-foot-in-front-of-the-other, one-day-at-a-time type of thing. It must get easier because it couldn't possibly get any harder.

But I'll never rat them out. I just need to give Clog enough and pretend to be co-operative. I just wish there was someone I could turn to.

∞

"It's the formula of poverty. Get pregnant at fifteen, marry, and have two more children before the divorce. Her struggling with minimum wage, groping hands, only to settle with an even bigger creep by twenty-five. Have another kid. Have another divorce. Possibly finish it off with a few miscarriages, a few abortions, and a surprise baby at thirty-five. By then, she'll be a grandmother watching the cycle repeat itself." Jason took a long drink. It was the same story he told anyone who was willing to listen. He had refined it into poetic prose that worked well in a redneck bar with country music blaring in the background and big guys hunched over their beer.

Jack liked redneck bars and was enjoying Jason's company. It made him feel slightly less miserable. In fact, he felt like a blue chip, top drawer mover and shaker compared to some of these patrons. He sipped his beer and continued listening to Jason.

"I knew the story but I was in love, and she was the type of beauty that makes your heart beat faster just thinking of her. There was no reason or logic, just the raw desire." Jason was talking to himself, staring into his beer and nodding. He turned to Jack. "Know what I mean?"

"Yeah," sighed Jack. "I know what you mean. I just got dumped by my fiancé."

"Hey, man, that's the shits. I mean, you must be feeling like shit."

"Hmph," Jack snorted, half-smiling. "You could say that. I'm still trying to get my head around this new reality."

"You screw around or did she?"

"I didn't screw around. And I don't think she did either."

"Couldn't get it up?"

Jack laughed. He didn't say anything and just clinked his glass against Jason's. He may not have been the most eloquent, but his heart was in the right place. "Another round? On me."

"You bet," Jason said. "Thanks."

Jack placed the orders and looked around. The bar was set out in a square with a wooden flap that allowed the barman and waitresses in and out. Bottles sat stoically in front of a mirror on glass shelves. Three one-arm bandits along the wall waited for those gambling enthusiasts who just couldn't survive a moment without throwing away their money. There was a disco ball above a dance floor to create a party atmosphere in the evening. It was two o'clock in the afternoon and there was just Jack, Jason, the bartender, and another couple in the room. On the whole, the place looked as it should. Not too shiny, not too clean. It did what it said on the tin: it was a place to drink, get drunk, and maybe meet some friends.

Jack decided he liked it there.

∞

Jack began popping into the Palomino Club after class on a regular basis. He would stay for a drink or two and then go home to study and get ready for the next day. Then he started to stay longer on Fridays, which extended to Thursdays and Fridays. Eventually, he started to skip classes and just stay from lunch to closing time. It impacted his grades and he didn't care. He managed to scrape by during his first semester. He was spending his student loan on booze but didn't give it a second thought.

He was in the middle of a decent Friday night session when he noticed Sarah walk in. She must have noticed him too because she turned her head away. He started to make his way to her when he saw her arm around another guy. She seemed happy, and the guy seemed decent enough. He was clean-cut and looked like husband material. She had cut Jack out of her life completely. No phone calls, no emails, no texts, no regrets. He arrived in the apartment one day a few weeks after she punched him in the face to see all of her clothes, furniture, and even cutlery removed. Her toothbrush was gone. Her perfume, makeup, and her pictures on the wall. Everything. She left the pictures of the two of them, and took the rest.

"Is that her?" Jason asked. He was Jack's barstool buddy these days.

"Yeah. Beaming with some new guy. Like she never even knew me. Like we never lived together for two years. You know, Jay, it makes me sick just to look at them."

"Why don't you go over and give her a piece of your mind?" Jason liked a good scene, preferably ending with a fight. He turned his glass on end, indicating to the waitress he was out of booze.

"Another one?" The waitress addressed Jack.

"Please. Double whiskey. With a beer."

"Me too," said Jason.

"Coming up."

"You get much studying done today? I noticed your books aren't even open," Jason said.

"I closed them when Sarah came in. I figured it was going to be one of those nights. Best get drunk. Up for that?"

"You bet. I'm not here for the dancing, but I do like those cowgirl outfits," Jason said.

"Agreed. I think we should start a judging contest. Determine the perfect outfit. Tight jeans are a must, but the skill is in the top. Too tight, too showy, too slutty. It's an art to get it just right." He lifted his glass. Jason drank to that.

"Excuse me son. I need a word with your boy-friend." A hand clasped Jason's shoulder and walked him away. He offered no resistance.

"Hi Jack. Miss me?"

Jack took his eyes off Sarah and turned his head.

"Good evening, Detective Clog, sir." Jack gave a mock salute and forced himself to relax.

"I see you're enjoying yourself, Jack. I hope this environment doesn't adversely affect your grades. You wouldn't want to upset mommy and daddy, would you?" He was looking directly at Jack. Clog was wearing jeans and a grey collared shirt but with a soft leather jacket like a mobster or undercover cop from an eighties TV show.

"I'm doing okay in school. I've been under a lot of pressure lately, you being top of the list."

"That's about to change."

Jack was encouraged. "Why? Have you decided to leave me alone?"

"No. Just the opposite. And I think you know why," Clog said. He moved his gaze to scan the room. Habit, probably.

"I haven't been home for a while. That's why I haven't been in touch. And I've been studying…"

"Yeah, I can see that," Clog said, nodding to Jack's books next to the table full of drinks.

"I have been studying. I'm just not coping as well as others."

"You're going to need to get a tutor because things are going to get a lot more difficult for you very quickly."

Jack's heart sank. "What happened now?"

"I think you know, but let me re-educate you. You agreed to inform me of anything going on with your parents. Now, I just found out yesterday that your parents haven't been heard from in months. They have some programmed noises to keep the ears busy but someone finally clicked and realised it wasn't real. Then we sent a team over to recon the property. No-one and nothing."

Jack reached for his beer. All of a sudden he noticed that his throat was dry. Parched. He took a long, slow drink and put the glass back carefully.

"Now, I appreciate that you're a serious student, a model academic, but even you must have wondered why you haven't seen or heard from your parents in such a long time. We would know if they called you because we have your phones bugged. We would have noticed if you showed up at the house, but we have nothing. I would call that odd. I would also call it a coincidence that greatly favoured your parents. But not me. And definitely not you."

Jack started to speak but didn't get anything out.

"Jack!"

He turned his head towards the sound. The bar was getting loud and even basic conversations needed to be shouted. But this was a woman's voice and he had heard it before.

"Jack! It's me!" A shape pushed past the standing figures and made its way to the edge of Jack's table.

"Carey?" She looked stunning. He had never seen her in anything but yoga sweats and occasionally the smart-casual demanded of offices and presentations. But tonight she looked like something out of a movie. She wore tight faded jeans and some weathered light brown cowboy boots and a top that was so corny in its bright red and white tassels that somehow it looked great. It was all topped off with a cowgirl hat slightly tilted back to show a beaming face, wide smile, and those two beacons of eyes that could hypnotise a bull at fifty yards.

"Sorry, gentlemen, I have a dance to collect on!" She grabbed Jack and hauled him to the dance floor before another word could be spoken. Detective Clog and his minder just looked on, unable to do anything without escalating matters unnecessarily.

"Thanks!" Jack leaned in to shout over the raunchy honky-tonk song that got all the women and men in the bar onto the dance floor.

"Looks like you needed to get out of there and I needed to get you here!" She smiled and threw her head back with a whoop and joined the mass of people dancing. Jack struggled to keep up.

"I've been watching you," she said.

"What?"

"I've been watching you these last few months."

"Spying on me?"

"No, silly, I'm just curious. I thought you'd get back with Sarah. Sorry about that." She nodded at Sarah and the new guy.

"Yeah. The shits."

"Friends of yours?" she asked, looking at Clog.

"Not exactly."

"Wanna dance?"

"Aren't we already?"

"Then let's pick up the pace!"

The honky-tonk song was followed by an even wilder one that whipped up the whole bar. There was a reason the Palomino was so popular. They had a great live band that knew how to work the crowd. It would slowly raise the tempo over their set until it reached a fevered pitch. Just when people couldn't go on much longer, they would cut it back to a slow dance and then take their break.

When it came time for the slow dance, Carey put herself in Jack's arms. His blood was pumping and he liked the way she felt next to him. He stole a glance towards Sarah. She was in her new man's arms. For some reason, it didn't hurt him so much with someone of his own to hold. Carey's body felt the music and Jack found himself relaxing and falling into the rhythm. Sarah fell away, Clog fell away, his parents fell away. He just swayed, moved his feet a bit, and felt Carey's body next to him. Her head was on his shoulder and one of her arms was slowly stroking his back. He had one arm on her lower back and found himself pulling her towards him. She didn't resist. His other hand cradled the back of her head and slowly traced her neck and shoulder.

When they made their way from the dance floor back to his booth, Clog and his goon were gone.

∞

Carey and Jack kissed that night outside of the bar. Not more, just a real kiss. He knew at that precise moment what Joe meant about finding a woman who could challenge him. Carey wanted more. Jack wanted more. But right then, they both knew. It gave Carey a tingle, and it gave Jack a shudder that sobered him stone cold. She was no ordinary girl and this was no ordinary kiss. It was their first kiss, and they didn't want it to be their last.

Chapter Five

Holding Pattern

"Did you book our tickets?"

"Yep. Just finalising payment and doing the check-in."

"Do you need my card?" Carey asked.

"No, I've got mine," Jack said.

"I can't wait! I've never been to Hawaii and everything I've seen of it is gorgeous.

"Hang on, Carey. There seems to be a problem. Your ticket went through but mine didn't."

"Is it the card? Here, try mine."

"No, I think it's something else. Let me try a different destination."

"But I thought we agreed to go to Hawaii," she said. She pouted a bit but it was just for show. Jack got a sense in their discussions leading up to this trip that the destination wasn't as important as the trip.

"I just entered the Florida Keys. Again, denied a ticket. Yours went through okay." He hesitated. "Maybe you'd like to go for a romantic drive with me instead and we'll have a picnic and stay in whatever hotel we find along the way?"

Carey took a deep breath and relaxed herself and shook off the disappointment. "I'd love to. As long as it's with you, I'd go anywhere." She didn't ask and Jack didn't offer a reason as to his trouble getting a ticket.

Jack wasn't having an exceptional semester but, since that night, he had curtailed his drinking and started studying again. He had a spring in his step and his marks fell into place. He was well placed to get a position with one of the local financial firms. He was in the top five percent of his class, was athletic, and presented well in a suit. He sent out CVs to the top twenty firms in the city. Not one was interested. Not even one interview. *Clog,* he thought to himself.

Jack eventually realised he must have been placed on the no fly list. He had to assume, then, that he was also put on the terrorist watch list, which meant that it would be easier for the CIA to track him globally and to put pressure on other governments to provide assistance. The result was that he was added to a list at the stroke of a button but couldn't be removed except by court order or due process. He was blacklisted and there was nothing he could do about it.

"Think, Jack, think," he said to himself. "If I were to run, what would my options look like? Could I take Carey? She's amazing but there's a limit to what she'd put up with. To remain undetected, I would need to get off the grid. Most likely alone. No computers, emails, mobile phones, regular phones, credit cards, drivers licence, passport, or ID of any form. I would need to avoid CCTV cameras because of facial recognition technology. While I am not an asset that the government wants desperately, these are things I should avoid. ATMs, police vehicles, and most businesses have cameras, but most are not tied into the central nervous system of the NSA—yet."

Jack's mind was racing through his options. He felt he would go mad if he didn't come up with a solution. And Carey just came into his life. *But she could leave as abruptly as Sarah*, his darker side reminded him. The tear on his heart was as painful as his need to be free from Clog. Combined, it was pushing him nearer to the edge of sanity.

Jack went through the reality of life on the run. "Cash and the ability to have or earn money will be crucial. Staying in hotels is out, as is renting a car. Both require a credit card and ID, and both have cameras.

"Work will be restricted to cash. I'd be a daily labourer. But would I need to resort to crime? Crime is tough; I don't think I could function where my only way to do so would be to steal from people. Would it be worth the risk? How would I sell the stolen goods?

Gold and jewellery is no good for me. I need to convert things into cash. And I'd think there are lots of snitches in that world. I don't think I'd make a good criminal.

"Say I manage to come up with a plan for cash, where do I sleep and stay off the radar? Do I stay in a big city and sleep on the streets, or integrate into the countryside as a labourer on a farm or ranch? Strangers will be suspicious of a stranger with no ID and no believable story."

Life on the run seemed just about doable, but was it sustainable? It would require a high degree of discipline and self-sacrifice. "And for what end? To exist another miserable day? Surely it can't be called living." He continued talking to himself, answering and responding.

"Perhaps staying and living with the humiliation of being the CIA's whipping boy is better. Let's assume I'm on the international terrorist watch list and the no fly list. I am not leaving the US unless I'm smuggled out of the country by foot or boat. That means Canada or Mexico. Canada is more likely, if only for the massive unguarded border and shared language.

"From Canada, I would do migrant labour work, hitch across the country, and either stow away on a big freight ship or talk my way in. There are fewer people in Canada and a less oppressive security infrastructure than the US. Assuming it can be overcome, where do I go? China? Russia? They may look upon me favourably because of what my parents did for them, but more likely, they wouldn't even know who I am. India is a great place to disappear but probably difficult to make money."

He ticked off the continents and countries. "Europe is overly sophisticated with their security, especially the UK. The Middle East is very strict on passports and a drifter would likely find themselves in jail. So what to do? Run or fight?

"Is fighting even an option? The CIA are the world's largest collectors of intelligence and probably the largest organised group of assassins. If I cross them, I am expendable. I will be killed with the memory of me expunged or re-written in a way that causes the fewest ripples. Even if I try to fight, what would a win look like? Killing Clog? Killing his team? They would see me coming a mile away. No, a win would mean getting out from under Clog's thumb. I have to believe that they are not all like him. Maybe I just need him removed. How? I need intelligence on his boss and the command structure. Where do I even begin to find this out? And what do I do in the interim? Live a double life? One where I spend every moment plotting revenge or resolution with Clog and the other as his loyal servant? How would that work? Could I get the leash loosened so I could fly and get a decent job?"

Jack pondered his options. "We all have our breaking point. What's mine? What will I do when I reach the point that defines who I am? Do I have the grit that can't be ground or do I become someone's meal? Fight or flight. Sometimes one has to run before he can fight. To higher ground, to advantageous ground, to any ground but the killing ground where he currently finds himself."

Jack was concentrating on every possibility. His body became increasingly tense. His fingers closed involuntarily into fists, white along the knuckles. His eyes bored into the table in front of him. His jaw clenched and relaxed, over and over. He had two options. One resulted in him being a dead man; the other, a zombie.

A hand gently caressed his shoulder and ran along the sinews of tensed muscle from his neck to his fists. Carey opened his hands and halted the stare. She took his head and turned it to her. She leaned forward and put a tender kiss on Jack's lips.

"Whatever it is, Jack, we can deal with it together. I am with you and I will help you. With anything. Just ask."

Just holding hands with Carey was sensual and exciting. She let him lead her. "I love you, Carey," he whispered.

"I know. And I love you more."

∞

Jack moved into her apartment within a month of their first kiss. Jack handed back the keys to his apartment and put his parents' house on the market to sell. They may have abandoned him, but at least they had the foresight to put the house in his name. He only discovered that when the tax bill and various utility bills started arriving. He figured he was entitled to a fresh start. He told Joe and was surprised at how calm he took everything.

"You've thought this through?" Joe asked. They went for a walk to avoid the eavesdroppers.

"Yes. I have no life here. My parents are on the run and I'm being crushed. Even if I end up working with Clog, I think my life is going to be pretty miserable."

"Well, you never know what tomorrow can bring and things rarely stay the same. People get promoted, priorities change, who knows. Don't panic."

"Easy for you to say."

"Life is surprising in many ways. It may surprise you yet."

"You're probably right, but right now I am finding it difficult to be positive."

"I understand, Jack. I really do. I'll keep an eye on the house for you in the interim. If you need any money, let me know. I've saved up for so many rainy days I have more than I need."

"Thanks, Joe, but I'll try to manage. I may still take you up on your offer."

"One word of advice, son," Joe said.

"Yeah?"

"Remember that you're not alone. When facing your enemies, build a team. Discover your weaknesses and plug those holes with people you can trust. In your case, find access to cash money and a place to stay when the heat gets too much."

They hugged and silently agreed to change the subject. They started talking about Joe's past and the rumours about him. Joe wasn't the bastard child of Einstein. The idea was so preposterous he chuckled at the thought of it. "Goes to show you that Goebel was right," he said.

"Who's Goebel?" asked Jack.

"One of Hitler's henchmen. He was part of the propaganda machinery. His famous idea was about the Big Lie: Tell a lie so outrageous, so unbelievable, and people will accept it as the truth—simply because no one would have the audacity to tell such a lie." Joe smiled.

"I don't follow."

"Let me ask you something. What have you heard about me around town?"

"That you keep to yourself, that you—"

"No, I mean what gossip have you heard about me?"

Jack blushed a bit and hesitated. "They say you are the son of Einstein."

"The *bastard* son of Einstein," Joe laughed. "Einstein was a lie, but making me a bastard made it believable."

"So you're not?"

"No," Joe laughed. "I'm as common as mud, but that's not why I lied."

Jack waited while Joe collected his thoughts.

"I was based in Korea and served through 'Nam. I rose through the ranks as a codebreaker but I requested to be nearer the action. Nothing glorious, just the same work but closer. But then I saw the men. Mangled in body and broken in mind. I saw what man could do to man. Eventually I had enough and I got transferred back to the US. I received my honourable discharge, even collected some medals and papers saying what a good soldier I was."

"Do you still have them?"

"In a steel box in a bank somewhere. They belonged to a different man. One day I woke up and decided to end my life. Not with a bullet, but by ceasing to exist as Max Harding and begin life as Joe Steinberg, bastard son of one of humankind's greatest scientists."

"So you just became someone else?"

"Yes, to a degree. I wanted peace. I wanted to be free of the dreams—nightmares—that never stopped. That's why I chose a small town in the middle of no-where."

Jack grinned. "Lucky me."

"Which leads me onto something else I need to tell you." Joe sounded nervous. His voice shook slightly.

"Are you alright, Joe?"

"Yes. I probably just need some sugar. Let's go in and have some hot chocolate."

It was Jack's favourite and the conversation turned to food, good drink and, of course, women.

As they drank their melted chocolate, Joe enjoyed the banter. *I just can't tell him he's my son. Not yet,* he thought to himself. *I thought I could. He deserves to know. But he's been through so much and he's just getting on his feet...* Instead, Joe said, "Have you decided what to do?"

"Yes." Jack put his finger to his lips to remind Joe: people were listening.

∞

When he returned to his shared apartment with Carey, Jack knew what he needed to do. He had decided to take Joe's advice—stay alive and live to fight another day, hoping that some tomorrow would make today worth living. Carey factored large in his thinking as did his desire to do something more with his life than just exist.

He pulled up the encrypted website Clog gave him and entered his password. He started typing:

Dear Detective Clog. I have had time to consider our arrangement and I can only apologise for my lack of compliance to date. This has all been so new to me. Then I felt the consequence of my non-compliance. I don't know what you did but my life is unliveable. You win. I give up. Tell me what you want. I haven't seen my parents since they ran. I don't know what I have that could be of use to you.

Sincerely,

Jack

He re-read it and pressed 'send'. He didn't have long to wait. Within the hour, he received a reply. "Give me something good, something new, and I'll ease up on you." It wasn't signed or identifiable, but it was hope. What could he give Clog?

Chapter Six

Traitors?

"Look at him," beamed Denise. "He looks so handsome."

Denise and James sat in the second last row on the left hand side of the auditorium. Jack was receiving his diploma in commerce, with distinction. Their little boy was all alone on the stage next to the dean and the faculty and a row of other notables behind them.

"Maybe we can sneak a little hello and give him a big kiss?" She looked at her husband. She was in physical pain watching this and not being a part of it. James kissed her and squeezed her hand. It was impossible but she needed to say the words.

"Oh, look. That must be his new girlfriend." She smiled at the word. "She's very pretty. And there's Joe." She was quiet as a lifetime of memories flooded over her. Did James not feel the same?

She turned to him. His hand rested on her knee and she held his hand. "I don't care what happens to us. We need to talk to him—if only to tell him that we love him and that we aren't the traitors he may think we are." It was unusual for Denise to speak like this but these were unusual circumstances.

"Let's see," he said. "We've turned people all over the world. We shouldn't be afraid of our son." They vowed to find a time and place to make that possible. Denise settled in more comfortably into her seat. She wanted to savour this moment.

∞

James applied a liberal amount of syrup on his pancakes. He liked the fluffy empty calories alongside some runny eggs. It was decadent and reminded him of easier less complicated times. It was the breakfast his parents would cook on a Sunday. His dad would get the glory of flipping and presenting them, although his mom made the batter and cleaned up afterwards. His mom made the best soft basted eggs in the world. She used a lot of butter and the eggs sizzled and popped in the cast iron pan. At just the right moment, she would add some water and put a lid on the pan. The eggs were never turned over and the top layer of the whites and yellow sealed up perfectly. Occasionally, he would have one pancake with one egg on top, which he would puncture and allow the yellow to flow freely into the spongey pancake. He would then add syrup on top of it to create a yellowy soup. His mom would say he was ruining his food but his dad just smiled and tussled his hair. Then he would copy his son, pouring syrup on his eggs and pancake.

Denise would have some toast and a coffee. She still had a fantastic body and was proud of it. She would constantly tell James he was going to get fat and become diabetic if he kept eating that way. Today, she just ate quietly.

"We're a long way from San Francisco, baby," James said, smiling at Denise. They met at a party in San Fran' in the summer of '68. They were young, alive, and free. They dressed like hippies, lived like hippies, and loved like hippies. When they first met, they noticed a gravitational tug of more than just the next tote or fumble. They actually liked each other. They started talking and found themselves enjoying being with each other more than anyone else. Soon they were exclusive and discovered that the hippie movement was a phase they had outgrown. James was twenty-two and Denise was twenty but they were soul mates and had the wisdom to not mess with that kind of magic. Others would scoff at them and call them prudes and squares. It was difficult at times.

"Those were crazy times," Denise said. "Do you regret our decision?"

The decision was June 21, 1972. That was the day they agreed to join the CIA. They were recruited by a grey non-descript guy who could see them for who they were. They stood apart from the hippies and he felt they could do some good for their country.

"We thought we were the coolest, smartest kids in town," James said. He stirred his coffee. "The seventies were great. Exciting, scary, but great. I miss those times."

Denise put down her cup. "No, you don't. Those were scary times with even worse ahead in the eighties. Do you remember Sergei? I still have dreams that they're after us. If they ever knew the whole truth…" She let the sentence linger. She wasn't sure if *she* knew the whole truth.

"Yes, but without Sergei we wouldn't have been re-assigned to Group 29." James leaned back in his chair and looked into the distance. "Ah, those were the days. Reagan, Star Wars, Gorbachev, Glasnost, Bush, the Wall, the mass migration of peoples in Europe, nuclear weapons for cash as the West bolstered Russia to ensure it didn't collapse, and most of all, our stationing back in the US."

Group 29 was significant in the British Army and the US Marines, but most of all, it was significant within the CIA. It was a secretive group within an organisation known for its secrecy. Only a handful of people knew of its existence and even fewer belonged to it. Denise and James were recruited by G29 after being made double agents for the then USSR by Sergei Andreevich Usilov. They officially became insiders, and yet they were unknown and expendable. No one would ever notice if they simply disappeared. It was Group 29 (or G29) that decided that James and Denise would settle down in a small town in the middle of nowhere in America's Midwest. That was 1990.

"What's brought this on? I haven't thought about this for ages," Denise said. "But it was anything but glamorous. What I remember best of that time was the birth of our beautiful boy Jack."

"I think that's what I'm trying to get at," James said. "In a very roundabout way."

James reached over and held her hand. It was a sensitive issue—especially as Jack wasn't James' biological son. What they didn't say was what happened to sow the seeds for their current exile.

In making their decision whether to see Jack again, their past came back to life. Their son was almost ten years old at the time and they had just stumbled onto the documents that triggered a series of events which eventually exposed them to Clog.

"Did you see the Hoffman dossier?" James' head was scouring over a table of paper. On it were legal foolscap folders with Top Secret stamped in red and a string to keep bundles of papers from spilling out. He leaned forward out of his chair to reach the articles near the far end of the table.

"Not yet. Anything interesting?" Denise had her own pile of papers to digest, mainly on people the agency was monitoring. She wanted to see how they could be best utilised. It was a bit like a 3D chess game.

"Possibly. It tracks Saddam Hussein's insistence of settlement in currency other than the US dollar for his country's oil. I didn't think much of it, but Hoffman's analysis was deemed of such paramount importance to the stability of the United States government that it was cited as sufficient to go to war over. Not Iraq's sale of oil for non-dollar currencies but the threat of other nations following suit. It was Vietnam all over again—but this time the domino theory applied to oil-exporting nations as a whole, with Iraq as an instigator."

"Okay," Denise said. "But so what? We didn't go to war over that. We went to War over weapons of mass destruction."

"Ostensibly, but Hoffman's dossier goes on to state that the government should find an alternative reason to invade and never to cite currency as a cause of open warfare."

"Not sure I agree. It's just one guy's view. Anyone else agree with him?"

"That's just it. There are a dozen experts all coming to the same conclusion and all of it is labelled 'eyes only'." James turned to Denise. "These are the documents our leaders would have seen in making their decisions."

"Okay, but it's only one factor. Like I said, we didn't go to war over the dollar." Denise put down her files and joined James at his table.

"Fair enough, but then there is this one expert's testimony, which puts all of this into question." James opened another 'eyes only' file with the name Telhorst. "This says more or less what the others say but with a certain reluctance. He makes reference to an organization, an order he calls it, that pulled the strings. He claims the order is primarily interested in the continuance of the US dollar as the anchor to the world's currencies. It was as though the experts were told what conclusions they needed to arrive at."

"Sounds spooky. Maybe he was drinking at the time, or possibly a bit paranoid? Or maybe just another think tank being given too much credit." Denise wasn't convinced.

"Listen to what he says: 'Absent gold as an anchor, the dollar represented the single most important stabilising factor in the world. It also was the mechanism by which this group was able to influence and control the major strategic decisions taken by the leaders of the integrated financial world. This, naturally, impacted every local sovereign nation, from its value of currency to foreign relations.' He seems to give this order a lot of credit."

James persisted and over the coming months unearthed a trove of top secret and eyes only files that pointed to the existence of a highly secretive group. A group of which even the G29 was apparently unaware.

James decided they would create their own digital dossier using a 1024-bit encryption service. They could store their findings without concern of others finding or questioning them on their motives.

"Remember all of the material we had on Bin Laden prior to 9/11? At the time he was just a former agent of the CIA in their opposition to the USSR in Afghanistan. What if this order and the information we have unearthed is the same type of thing? From what we can see, this group wants to create a new enemy of the United States to counterbalance its power."

Denise stopped her reading. "What type of group promotes the stability of the US dollar on one hand and openly tries to create an enemy for the US on the other? Psycho or brilliant? Whose side are they on?"

"Theirs, I think," said James. "And nations, borders, and ideologies seem to count for little or nothing to these people."

"Be careful, James. Perhaps we should consult with the higher ups?"

"Let's build our dossier first. I don't want to present any of this until we are completely certain. If we're wrong, we'll lose our jobs and maybe worse. If we're right, this is a serious threat to the national security of the United States. It's 2004 and the world is a very dangerous place."

It took until 2010 before they were able to make any headway with China. They allowed themselves to be recruited by China's Ministry of State Security at a low level. They were able to leverage this position to make contact with future leaders and their assistants. In this fashion, they met Wang Wei and were able to gain his trust in 2012. He wasn't turned, but he remained a valuable point of contact. Over time, he was appointed to his position within the most powerful office in the world, second only to the White House. Wang Wei became second assistant to the General Secretary of China.

There was no way for James or Denise to know this at the time, but a CIA mole reported back to Langley the existence of two Americans who had been turned and were now working for the MSS. It was this accidental information that led Detective Clog to discover they were also working for the FSB (formerly KGB). It was only on reflection months later that James and Denise narrowed down their exposure to this event. As agents, it was the risk they took and thus far they had been lucky enough. But this event had led to Jack's dislocation and the pain and suffering he was forced to endure due to no fault of his own.

It was this sense of injustice that eventually tipped the balance for James and Denise to meet up with Jack again.

Chapter Seven

Triple Agents?

"I never understood why a bottle of scotch—or any premium spirit—was built so tough." Jack lay in bed with Carey, the morning light just visible on the edges of the blinds that covered their bedroom window. He saw the empty champagne bottle standing vertical on the dressing table but his thoughts were drawn to the half full bottle of premium scotch lying just beyond reach next to him. His graduation diploma, received the day before, sat on the table next to the closet.

"Hmmm?" Carey was in that wonderful place in the morning when the heat of the covers balances perfectly with the cold from the open window. She didn't open her eyes. They had drunk a lot last night and usually neither of them suffered from hangovers—but she did notice a bit of a fuzzy helmet (as she called her minor hangovers) on the mornings after excessive drinking sessions. The best cure was to stay in bed as long as possible.

Jack continued his thought process. "These bottles look like any other bottles, but they aren't. They were designed and built to fall a certain distance, like the few feet from a bed onto a carpet or even a wooden floor. They could fall six feet or more before you needed to worry."

"Shuddup," mumbled Carey. She had patience for most of Jack's nonsense but sometimes he could go on forever if someone didn't nip it in the bud.

"Just checking if you were awake and ignoring me." Jack slipped out of bed and made his way to the shower. Hot water was always a good way to reset his engines on a morning like this. He would then make some coffee and toast and bring them to Carey. Neither of them had work this morning and he wanted her to rest.

He brushed his tongue thoroughly, flossed, and then rebrushed his teeth. He thought about how ridiculous it was to brush one's teeth before drinking coffee in the morning. He shrugged and carried on. Habit.

After he showered and performed the normal morning bodily functions, he went to the kitchen to make some coffee. He liked grinding his own beans when he had time. The oily beans were turned into ultra-fine grounds, which he then put into a pot with a name that always eluded him. It was originally of Italian design when aluminium was all the craze. It consisted of two parts with the water in the bottom half, a steel filter and a top part. The ground heaven was put into the filter bit and the two parts were screwed together. You then put this pot on your hob or oven top (or fire if camping) and let the heat turn the water into steam. This steam would pass through the ground heaven and create a liquid heaven in the top part of the pot. It was pure espresso and was probably meant to be consumed in small quantities. Jack poured himself a large mug of the stuff, probably the equivalent to eight shots. At times he would drink it black. Sometimes he would heat up some milk. Today he added cream (which he warmed so as to not ruin the liquid heaven). Not a lot, just enough to make it decadent and take off some of the edge.

As he poured his cream into his mug, he decided to let Carey sleep. She didn't need to be up and would probably appreciate the sleep more than the romantic gesture of coffee and crumbs in bed. He closed the door to the kitchen so his movements didn't wake her and settled into the upright wooden chair next to the table. The outside world was waking up and he could see the sun striking its 8:30 pose. All of the working people had left and the children were being bundled into cars to be ferried to school. They lived within walking distance of Carey's work in a little grouping of streets that still had greenery and families living in them. The government buildings sat on imposing grounds across from a large museum, which was next to an equally imposing building housing the headquarters of the country's largest insurance company. Carey's office was on the other side of the government buildings next to the Land Registry and Companies House offices and within a stone's throw of the state's five largest law firms.

His eyes closed slowly like a contented cat. He exhaled and then inhaled the heavenly aroma from his mug. The cream covered his lips and tongue and roof of his mouth. It was the delivery agent for the much needed caffeine. He had already had a lot of water, but this was medicinal. His eyes slowly opened as he returned his mug to the table. *This morning is turning out to be just what the doctor ordered*, he thought.

Just then his hands became clammy as a jolt of electricity brought him out of his reverie. His right eye flickered and adrenaline began coursing through his body. He stood up and walked to the front door. On the other side were the two people he needed to see more than anything in the world. His parents.

The flood of emotions and adrenaline and fear and anger and excitement were almost too much. Nothing was said. Jack put his fingers to his lips and motioned them to stay where they were. He quickly wrote a note and left it on the table for Carey in the event she awoke before he returned. He put on a light jacket and slipped on his sandals and the three of them went for a walk.

It was a full three blocks to the park and they walked the first one in silence. They wanted to hug each other but had to hold back. Jack didn't think he was under constant surveillance, but he knew his house was bugged. No one would recognise his parents where he lived with Carey but there was also no reason to be overtly friendly either. Too much emotion would be remembered by the more nosey neighbours—and there were plenty of those.

When they were in the clear, they all hugged and kissed each other. Denise had been silently crying from the moment the door opened and Jack felt her tears against his cheek as she held him tight. James looked anxious but pleased at the family reunion. He knew that Denise and Jack needed this time, and he did too. But he also knew they didn't have an unlimited amount of it. He wanted to sit down and debrief Jack, and at the same time establish a means of contacting each other in the future.

"Have you had any further trouble from the CIA?" James asked eventually. They had settled into the swing set with Jack in the middle and Denise and James on either side.

"They have me on the no-fly and terrorist watch lists," Jack said. "They blocked me from getting a proper job and are making my life difficult. I eventually said I would co-operate with them. The only problem is that means betraying you. In short, they are making my life very difficult."

"They are the original bastards," James said. "It's siege warfare. They surround their target and starve him out until he yields. Don't worry, everyone breaks."

"I'm not breaking, I'm just buying time. I have a plan," Jack said.

"Don't do anything rash, Jack," Denise said.

"I'm not, Mom. I just need to give them something. Anything."

"How about giving them what they want?" James said.

Denise looked at James. She nodded, guessing where this was headed.

"Jack, we're also CIA."

At this, Jack's legs went straight and he stopped swinging. "Then just get them to tell Clog to back off."

"It's not as easy as that, son. We're part of a group that doesn't officially exist. If caught, we would be dis-avowed. There will be no records, no history, no rescue."

"But Dad, there must be some way to clear your name."

"Sorry son, but that's not how it works."

"Maybe there's another way," said Denise. "Maybe we give him the dossier and let Jack take the credit?"

"But that'll put him in even more danger," James said. "If he thinks things are rough now, he'll just end up dead."

"I think I'll take my chances," said Jack. "Besides, I don't like the idea of being Clog's whipping boy until one of us dies. What's in this dossier?"

James and Denise decided to tell Jack what they had been working on for the last ten years and how they came to know a young Chinese rising star who may be able to help.

"The enemy of your enemy is your friend, huh?" Jack said.

"Something like that," Denise said.

"Will it work?" Jack said.

"We can only try," James said.

"How do I stay in touch with you going forward?" Jack said.

"Let's use an encrypted site. Maybe the same one you use with Clog. You can tell him you suggested it and that you managed to get all of this information out of us."

"Whatever you do, don't tell him everything," Denise said. "Don't tell him you have the dossier, just some of the information from it. If this Chinese guy is the right person, share enough with him so he can do something about it."

"What's in the dossier? How will I know what's the right stuff?" Jack asked.

"You'll know. Just be careful. It involves the most powerful people in the world you probably haven't heard of. And a few everyone has. The consequences impact every transaction around the world, from buying a tank to a pack of chewing gum. We can't talk in person until this is over. It's too dangerous for you. Especially now. We'll monitor the site daily. If you need anything or require answers, ask us online."

"You'll need to ask Clog to meet our Chinese contact somewhere other than in the US. Dubai is the usual place but try for somewhere in Europe. Germany or the UK are good places," James said.

"Is he that important?" Jack said.

"Yes. He's very important to us now that the CIA is after all of us. It's important that Clog gets you off the no-fly and terrorist watch lists. Flying to another country should do that. Also, this asset we want you to meet is the only link to a power sufficient to counter the CIA's."

"Will he bite?" Jack said.

"When you read the dossier, you'll understand. He'll be salivating. Big time," James said. "He'll bite your hand off to co-operate. It affects him personally as well as his country. If he plays his cards right, he could be a big player in China and the world in the future."

"If it goes according to plan," said Denise, "he'll allow you to keep in contact with us and we can guide you through the process. There's a lot to do."

"But I don't want to betray you."

"If this works, you won't be."

∞

When Detective Clog first received the encrypted message, his heart sped up for a second. He was intrigued and agreed to meet up.

"Hi Jack."

"Hi. Do you want a coffee?" They were meeting at a greasy spoon. Neither of them had been there before. Jack already had a coffee in front of him.

"Sure. Three sugars, two creams."

Jack went to the cashier and ordered the coffee. It was a hybrid shop, somewhere between a comfy coffee shop and cafeteria. Everything was displayed so you could order and eat without speaking much English at all. Pictures of breakfasts and lunches filled the walls behind the counter. All you needed to do was point and grunt. The trays and plates were stacked up at one end and you would graze along the counter until you reached the end. Jack returned to his booth and handed Clog the coffee, three sugars, two creams.

"So you've made some progress?"

"Yeah. My parents came around and visited me. It was a total surprise."

Clog nodded.

"It didn't go as I anticipated."

Clog's eyebrows raised. He didn't say anything.

"They were happy to see me and they were quick to explain their point of view on things. It was weird," Jack paused. "They started going on about being part of the CIA and that they had stumbled onto something huge and needed my help. They are in cahoots with the

Russians and the Chinese, both of which think they are working for them. They are in such a muddle…" His voice trailed off.

"The Chinese *and* the Russians? Are you sure?" Clog was interested. Very interested. This had become unexpectedly big. True triple agents were things of the past and the capture or cooperation of one would be a major asset for him and his team. "What's this about being part of the CIA?"

"That's what they said. Are you able to check it out?"

"First thing after this conversation. You bet." Clog took a sip of his coffee. It was absent-minded and automatic. He wet his lips, paused with cup mid-air, and then took another sip. The coffee was good. Better than he expected.

"What do you want me to do?"

Clog was pleased to see his techniques had worked. Jack was fully on his side, devoid of any delusions of familiar loyalty. Clog believed himself tough but fair. Jack had survived the tough Clog and now he would see the fair side of him. "I want you to become as close as possible with them. Agree to whatever plan they want you to do and keep me informed. We'll have to play things by ear."

"Okay. And what about my job? I was accepted to a position and I don't want to hurt my career more than it has already been." Jack remembered the black listing and the cold shoulder he had received from the firms he applied to. It took joining Clog's team and total submission before the doors started opening again.

Clog worked to restrain any movement that would betray the satisfaction he felt. "I think you'll be okay. Trust me on that one."

"I trust you. And what happens if I need to travel abroad? They mentioned something about meeting this young Chinese guy. I assume this means going to China or something."

"You go where they tell you to go. I'll ensure you have travel arrangements and security clearance to get where you need to go."

Jack's hands were wrapped around his coffee mug. He took a sip, put the cup down, nodded, and left the café.

Clog took another sip. *Good coffee*, he thought.

Chapter Eight

A Butterfly's Wings

Back at Carey's apartment, Jack dumped his cold coffee and noticed to his satisfaction that Carey was still sleeping. He pulled out his laptop, made another coffee and started reading the dossiers his parents put together. He was paranoid and ensured no copies remained on his computer. He read using the encrypted site and made notes in another saved encrypted folder. *His* dossier, newly created.

He managed to read just over two hours' worth of his parent's dossier. Carey had woken and he put aside his work. It took almost two weeks before he was able to piece together some of the history behind his predicament.

When he pieced together the Chinese element, he concluded that everyone was connected. Like the beating of a butterfly's wings which cause a typhoon halfway around the world. There were two butterflies in question, insofar as Jack was concerned, the first of which was halfway around the world and twelve years earlier. In a time prior to Clog or Carey or Sarah. In a time when he was still a boy.

∞

Hangzhou, China

12 years earlier

The Golden Rule: He who has the gold, rules.

"If a seed falls to the earth and grows into a mighty oak, do we say the earth is the master of the tree?"

A young man, just older than a boy, thought and then replied, "Does not the earth benefit from the decaying leaves and branches and eventually the tree itself?"

"Yes, wisely put. But the tree benefits even more. It grows and lives centuries, draining nutrients from the soil and sky alike. The soil merely holds it firm and allows it to grow."

"But the earth always wins," said the student.

"Yes, but so does life. And without life, the earth is reduced to merely a rock hurtling through space around and amongst other rocks."

The teacher used his walking stick to draw a circle in the ground and then put a curved line within it. "Do you know what this is?"

"Of course," replied the student. "Yin and Yang. The push and pull of all things."

"Very good." Professor Han smiled and put his hand on the shoulder of his favourite student. Wang Wei was only fourteen but he grasped the fundamentals quickly. He would be a good ruler someday—if it was meant to be.

"Life comes in all forms," Han continued. "From the largest animal on land and sea to the smallest insects. All benefit the earth and all provide their remains to future life by returning to the soil. They make grass and food for all the animals, great and small."

Wei looked at the wizened man. Han had a long beard, but most of his face was bald like the top of his head. Large patches on his cheeks had no hair at all. The white hair and beard fell carelessly from Han's head to sit on his shoulders and chest. He wasn't fat but he wasn't skinny either. He was tall and big. His clothes were simple: the customary robe of the educated. His walking stick was extraordinary with a large globe on the top carved out of what was once a large knot on a branch. Wei liked Professor Han. He wasn't like the modern teachers. He was like someone from a different era.

"Do you understand what I am saying?"

"Yes, sir." His voice was between that of a boy and a man, sometimes betraying his youth. His mind, though, was anything but infantile.

"Then listen carefully. We call this balance in nature 'harmony'. No one is master of the other, yet all are interdependent. It is a symbiotic relationship. It may be that the earth can kill us and we may someday be capable of killing her, but for both or all of us to live, we must be in balance."

"Yes, Professor. You make it sound easy."

"Yes, but here comes the tricky bit. Apply this to life as we know it and see what we can learn from it. Yours is a new world, very different from mine. My life—and our history as a people—has been one of power and war and uncertainty. This is a constant in life, but you and your generation will face a new test. It is a powerful force and the West has perfected it."

"What is it?" Wei became frightened.

"You know that China is an ancient people with a proud heritage in science, math, and the arts. We were rich and powerful and circumnavigating the globe when the West was still debating whether it was flat or round."

Wei grinned. He was proud of China and knew that it would be great again.

"But amidst the chaos arose some technological advances that allowed them to conquer the globe, including us to an extent."

"But that was over a century ago," Wei said. "We have become strong again. Our leaders have saved us from the capitalists and made us safe."

Professor Han was silent. Chairman Mao and the others had been dead for quite some time and yet their ghosts still loomed large. "China is waking up and it will be strong again. But you must learn everything you can about the greatest secret weapon of the West if you have any hope of success with the future."

"What weapon is that?" Wei, like most fourteen-year-old boys, loved any weapon—especially a secret one.

"Finance. Money. Currency."

"Oh," Wei said. The deflation in his voice was evident.

"Not 'oh'. You should say 'ah!' because that is the weapon they will use to enslave China. I will not be around to see it, but you will. I want you to remember this, even if you forget everything else I have taught you over the years. Promise me this?"

"But you haven't said anything yet." Wei regretted this the moment he said it. He felt the slap against the back of his head instantly. It was surprisingly firm for such an old man.

"We'll talk tomorrow when you're not so insolent." With that, Han hobbled off.

Wei wasn't pleased. His parents would hear about this and punish him a hundred times worse when he got home.

∞

It was a week before Han recommenced his lesson. He gave no warning and it seemed to have no connection to the previous topic, which was the excretions of a certain beetle in wild grass.

"Finance is like the earth. Some earth yields bountiful crops and some don't. The farmer can only do so much—add nutrients, chemicals, balance pH, drain, irrigate—but one has limitations outside of the farmer's control—sunlight, exposure, clay and stone content, and so on."

"So too with finance. I am not talking about your parents or your local bank or even a national bank. I am talking about the fabric, the essence of the system that the banks follow. I am not even talking about capitalist or socialist banking. Go to the very essence of finance: the idea of banking, venture capital, and underwriting debt—whether for building empires, fostering peace or war, or merely survival. Do you understand what I am saying?"

Chastened from the consequences of his earlier behaviour, Wei simply nodded.

"At this level, there is no one person or group that can control it, but there are many who try. In the West, a small number of people and organisations have managed to manoeuver themselves into a position of such power that they control the currencies of sovereign nations. The nations notionally control their currency but they are playing by the rules of this small group. This small group raises money, balances payments, and ensures that the wheels of commerce and industry are well oiled and functioning. All of this is fine except for a few minor points:

Money or capital, as with power, becomes more concentrated as you go up the pyramid. You must constantly ask, who sits on top? He (it is usually a man) does not seek publicity nor court favour. Yet favours and power are showered upon him in exchange for his approval.

Real power always rests in the masses and the natural resources of a country. In each system, the masses give their power to their leaders through some romantic feudal ideal of kings and lords or through the idealism of communism or democracy. Still others have their power ripped from them at the point of a gun. Dictators can only retain power in this fashion."

Wei was about to say something about China's not so distant history but thought better of it.

Han continued. "The point I wish to make is that the people in power eventually realise their fragile position so they begin enacting laws to reduce social mobility and extend their power. Each law removes freedoms from an otherwise peaceful citizenry. Eventually, everyday actions are made illegal and the citizenry are corralled into the desired mind-set of the elite. Power given by the masses to their leaders is rarely if ever returned. Only a revolution with clearly stated objectives can bring about the change that is sometimes required.

"Why is this relevant to you? Because this new form of Western finance takes the form of fertile ground into which you plant your seeds of desire. It then entraps you into accepting its terms and waits while you dig yourself a hole so deep you can't get out. Its stated objective is to lend you the maximum amount of money so you can better your lives, be healthier, better educated, and travel the world."

"Isn't that a good thing?" Wei asked.

"Rarely does human nature pursue or become satisfied with what is good for it. China, if it is not very careful, will fall prey to the West and find itself unable to exercise its sovereign will without first consulting its paymasters—the cabal of international financiers who smile, are well mannered, and have a long term strategy. Many in the lower levels of high finance are obsessed with quarterly results and relative performance—they are merely part of the fabric and not one of the weavers. The West fears an independent China capable of standing alongside the euro and dollar as world reserve currencies."

Wang Wei listened to his master patiently. He could still feel the cane his father hit him with as a result of the previous week's insolence. When Han finished, Wei tried to say something clever.

"I think I understand, but I will need time to fully grasp the meaning and extent of your words." Wei paused. "How can I place myself to help China against this threat from the West?"

Han smiled. "You study. You learn. And you go into politics. I still have contacts at the highest levels. I will ensure that you get fast-tracked towards leadership, where your decisions and actions will have the greatest impact."

Wang Wei was delighted to hear those words. He knew he could be a leader. At that moment, he refrained from smiling and gave his professor a nod of gratitude in a way that acknowledged Han as the master and Wei as the student. "Thank you, Professor Han. You give me great honour and pride with your words. I will do my best to live up to your expectations of me."

Han clasped a hand on Wei's shoulder and started walking. Their lessons would continue and his student had just made a life-decision that required them to redouble their efforts if he was to reach greatness. Of that, Han had no doubt.

∞

Jack was able to weave the past onto the present in light of recent events. Everyone had seen it on television. Now he was looking at it in a dossier, complete with photos of the main players. He couldn't believe what he was reading.

He could visualise Wang Wei stepping aside on that fateful day as the General Secretary walked by. It had been over a decade since that talk with Professor Han and Wei could still remember every word. There was an intensity with Han that day, an earnestness to distil his wisdom and pass it to Wei. Wei was fast-tracked through his schooling and military duty to get this job. He was now second assistant to the General Secretary of China. It was an honour, but it was a lot of work. He wanted to help China become the power in the world that it deserved to be, and he knew that control over their currency was essential to achieving that.

"Don't just stand there, get a move on." The handlers for the event didn't mince words—even if the ear they bashed had the ear of the General Secretary.

"Where do you want me?" Wei said in the direction of the voice.

At that moment, the first assistant arrived. Her name was Ni La. Wei liked her but feared her even more.

"Wang." It was a bark. "You aren't needed here now. Try to get some rest and I'll see you in the office tomorrow."

Wei wasn't sure he heard right. Rest? See you tomorrow? Their jobs didn't include the luxury of sleep and, as far as he knew, she didn't care if he got hit by a train. Since when was she so polite? Wei didn't dwell on it and grabbed a coffee off the table on his way out. It felt like a holiday.

The next morning, Wei awoke to banging on his door. His phone had twenty-three missed calls. "Damn," he thought. "Must've had it on silent. No wonder I slept so well."

He got up and clicked open the lock on the door. It was pushed in immediately by a group of military police.

"Hey!" Wei said as the uniformed hard-ass pushed past him. He heard the sounds of rummaging. Something fell and broke. It sounded heavy. Probably his coffee mug.

"Get dressed and come with me," the MP said.

"What is this?" Wei was used the gruffness of the Red Army's MPs. At least they were police and not some grunt soldier. MPs were tough as nails but fair. Soldiers were tough as nails but had no latitude for thought. Wei didn't like accidents—especially involving live rounds of ammunition and his head.

"I'll brief you on the way. There has been an incident."

"Incident? What happened?"

"The General Secretary has been shot. He's still alive but in critical condition. The first assistant Ni has been arrested. She has confessed."

Wei froze with his T-shirt and towel still in his hands. His mouth must have opened but nothing came out.

"You'd better hurry," said the MP.

Wei snapped out of it and quickly got dressed. He pulled on his uniform trousers, pre-ironed shirt, and was buckling his belt and walking with his shoes untied as the door clicked closed behind him. Soon he would find out if he also was going to 'confess' as Ni La had.

When he arrived, he found there was no firing squad nor kangaroo court. Ni La had conspired to kill the General Secretary. They briefed Wei and he answered their questions in a daze, affixed to a polygraph test for good measure. When they finished with him, he began to ponder his future in politics. At least he didn't get the bullet. Where would they assign him and would this shame and dishonour haunt him his entire life?

∞

Jack didn't have the complete picture, but he put together what he could gather from the facts set out in the dossier. There was a young man who was groomed by the establishment within China to be a leader. Denise and James came into contact with this man on the basis that they could use him as an asset in the future. In the interim, the CIA became aware of his parents and there was an attempt on the life of the leader of China.

Jack made the pertinent notes and kept digging. He hadn't yet determined his next step.

Chapter Nine

Illuminati

It was almost a week before Jack came across the core of the conspiracy he was facing. It was like the earlier butterfly, but much more distant—in time as well as circumstance. But it fluttered its wings nonetheless with a consequence that impacted his parents, and his own life. This conspiracy was the driving force behind the oft-quoted new world order. Prior to reading the dossiers, he thought any mention of the new world order was the remit of nutcases and racists. Armed with the knowledge that these were dossiers created at the highest levels of intelligence within the CIA, he had no option but to recalibrate his sense of reality.

∞

Bavaria, 1780

How do you enforce a loan against a king?
Fund his enemy.
If he doesn't have an enemy, create one.

"So many of us assume we are somehow special," Costanzo said to the well-dressed gentleman. "And then there are those of us who are, in fact, unique." He smiled and drank deeply from the stein of beer in front of him.

Adolph smiled at the inference that he was included in that group. He had big plans to change the world around him but was stifled at every turn. He had joined the Freemasons at the earliest opportunity and had reached as high as he could, yet he still had no influence.

"What can I do to help you?" Adolph asked.

"You can join our order and help us implement plans, which happen to be similar to your own."

"Such as?"

"We simply wish to exchange enlightened thought among fellow enlightened members."

"And what do you call 'enlightened thought'?" Adolph asked. He was used to grand talk but realised recently that most people simply wanted to drink and have an excuse to talk nonsense with others who agreed with them.

"We would like to think without the censure of the Jesuits and Catholic Church, for a start. We would like to end the injustices visited upon us and people like us who want to improve the world. It's already 1780 and we are living like it's 1380." Costanzo Marchese di Costanzo was, in addition to being an infantry captain in the Bavarian army, a true liberal and didn't want his mind to be constrained by anyone—least of all by those lecherous priests and their corrupt pope.

Adolph took a drink and grabbed a handful of the crusty bread from the table. The flour was quite heavy on the crust and he tapped it on the wood table before taking a bite. "You say that but we need to remember the mind-set of most people. The majority believe in some version of the church—whether it's Catholic or Protestant. We should really try to attract the smartest and most enlightened, regardless of their religious beliefs."

Costanzo didn't like this but his instructions were to recruit Adolph Freiherr Knigge at all costs. He swallowed his reservations and did his best to ensure that his new recruit actually joined. "You probably know better than me. I am just trying to find the enlightened and invite them to join us."

"You have done your job admirably," joked Adolph. He put his arm around Costanzo in friendship. "Now tell me, what do you call yourselves?"

Costanzo looked furtively over his shoulder and said just above a whisper, "The Illuminati."

∞

The Illuminati, meaning 'the enlightened' in Latin, was founded on the 1st May, 1776, by Adam Weishaupt in Bavaria. He sought to surround himself with enlightened people such as Adolph Knigge to deal with the abuses of power in the state and church. Adolph's plan, adopted by Adam Weishaupt, was to use the infrastructure of the Freemasons to spread the influence of the Illuminati. He targeted the men who ran the lodges to promote and convert their members to join the new order. Their efforts were successful in Germany, Austria, and France, and impacted Freemasonry across Europe. Their objectives included the vision of a rationalist state run by philosophers and scientists while tolerating alchemy and mysticism by its members. The level of mysticism eventually led to dissent within the order.

The power and influence of the Illuminati extended into many of the top echelons of power within Germany and, increasingly, France and their neighbouring countries. Its detractors began to accuse it of having revolutionary and atheistic tendencies. The Illuminati evolved into a secret sect within Freemasonry. Its height of power corresponded with the expulsion of Adolf Knigge in 1784, the same year it was banned by the Bavarian ruler. By edict in 1785, all secret societies or orders were banned, which included the Illuminati. All available documents of or by the Illuminati were seized in 1786 and published in 1787. Weishaupt fled and the Order of the Illuminati was thought to have been crushed.

∞

The history of the organisation was very much at the forefront of the members as they sat in their annual meeting. While members met during the year, it was only annually or on emergencies that all 11 members sat around the same table or in the same room to discuss the matters at hand. On this day, the order needed to deal with an exceptionally successful member who wanted to expand the role of the organisation. It was up to one man to uphold the principles of the order.

"Mr. Roth, I understand what you are saying, but I have no intention of repeating the mistakes of our predecessors."

"We must be cautious now more than ever," said Roth.

"It's already 1892 and we are more powerful than ever before," said Cecil.

"Mr. Rhodes, we have achieved great things together and we all agree with your objectives of a grand empire bestriding the globe providing peace and stability. You have done wonders in Africa, but America is not yet ready to re-join any empire. By God, it's becoming one in its own right." Roth tapped the ash from his cigar and took another long draw. He didn't smoke except in these gatherings.

"If you just look at what we've achieved in Africa," Rhodes said. "The railways, the agricultural boom, the shear wealth of raw materials. It has the making of the breadbasket and money purse of the world. I anticipate the population booming from affluence and prosperity, exporting its excess food around the globe. Famine will be a thing of the past—especially so on the continent of Africa itself. And diamonds and gold will be so plentiful as to embarrass El Dorado."

"You make an eloquent appeal and you have our undying support, both financially and politically, but the world is not ready for your plans."

Rhodes scoffed. "Are we talking about the same group that fomented the French Revolution and inspired Karl Marx? Our group can and should do anything we see fit."

"Our order is no longer the Illuminati, Cecil," Roth said acidly. "If you wish to continue your meteoric climb, I would suggest you speak less and act more. We can't afford spies overhearing us. We gather together to act and not merely talk."

"Yes, Mr. Roth," said Rhodes. He was rarely humbled, but even a lion must defer to the elephant when their paths cross.

"Speaking of the Illuminati," said Sir George. "Did you know that the famous Goethe joined that Order? Marvellous. Simply marvellous."

"And it's why we have formed this new order. We mustn't cling to romantic notions of perceived past glory. We gather for results." Roth left the remainder of his cigar to burn in the tray. "Our family's bank has enormous financial and political clout. Combined with the other leading financial families of Europe, we have become virtually unstoppable. Provided we are able to keep our gatherings private, we should be able to minimise our collective losses and maximise opportunities, all while doing our patriotic duty to our respective nation hosts."

"Hear, hear!" a clear majority of the 11 members voiced their approval.

"But long term, we'll only survive if we remove ourselves from the spotlight and confine ourselves to influencing politicians and monarchs. We'll be able to determine the outcome of wars, save governments, and accumulate favours from the highest levels of monarchies, despots, and empire builders."

∞

Jack tried to piece together the conversations that provided the link from the current members to the ones over two centuries. There were only scraps of papers, second hand information and unguarded moments of clarity that provided him with the information he so desperately wanted to collate. The conclusion: there was a distinct and functional group of individuals who operated in the shadows with the sole purpose of furthering their objectives regardless of nation, allegiances or morality.

Jack noted that a century of influence had made clear to this order that the control of currency was as important and as powerful as the ability to create it. Sovereign countries could still create their money and spend it as they wished, but as all new currency is effectively debt, these sovereign countries would need to first seek approval from this group of financiers. *They wanted to become the toll keepers of all monies used regardless of geography*, Jack thought to himself.

Does this make a conspiracy or just the logical extension of efficient capitalism? Jack was forced to rethink his training thus far. Good banking is all about redirecting capital to where it can best be utilised. Those who control the direction of capital also decide where and for what it is to be used. Capital does not have a mind of its own; it is directed by the bankers, who buy sufficient bonds to fund a nation's war aims or peace drives or expansion dreams. Or it can starve a nation of fresh funds and force it into austerity and potentially internal crisis. *It may seem neutral in theory, but is far from it in practice,* Jack concluded.

The taming of the United States of America was the greatest feat by the financiers. While it was relatively easy to enslave somewhere like Argentina or wage currency wars on the European continent, it was a feat of contrariness to enslave a nation as powerful and creditworthy as the USA and reduce it over a century into a husk of its former self. In its place, the US became a military behemoth without equal alongside a population bloated on affluence and ignorance. *Yet it now holds the unenviable title as the world's largest debtor,* Jack mused. *Within those chains, the mighty behemoth was reduced to a tamed pet.*

Jack began to understand more as the history he was reading about in the dossiers become more recent. In some ways, it provided a parallel reality to everything he had read about in school.

A project undertaken since the end of World War II was the ever-closer union of the European powers—chief amongst them France and Germany but including the rest of the leading economies. It took forty years of treaties to achieve the imperfect euro. They had no idea that a third power would rise and dwarf all others that had come before: China.

The current objective of this group, Jack noted, is the inclusion of China into the financial fabric of its international finance. The US, as key mover in the world since WWII and the anchor for all currencies since 1971, has implemented a host of laws and regulations for the use and transmission of capital in the world, which will ensure that any nation that joins it will be subject to the same regulations. In this manner, China will find itself on the same road that the US chose a century ago. On a road with this secretive organisation acting as toll keepers.

Who is this group? Jack kept asking himself. He wanted names, addresses and photos. It didn't help him to suspect; he needed to know. In its present form, it is a group of enlightened men and women (but still predominantly men) who meet from time to time to discuss how to make the world a safer place. Their ideals are admirable but shrouded in secrecy. Even the name is unknown except to the most senior of members. Illuminati? No. The current Illuminati are a side show. This nameless group knows who its members are and operate with discretion. They return to their levers of power in the IMF, US Federal Reserve, the Bank for International Settlements, as well as the influential think tanks that direct policy in the West. They rarely take public office, preferring to be the power behind the throne. They are not elected, nor do they wish to be subjected to the scrutiny of public elections, but they look for the right people to stand in their stead. The right president or prime minister of this country, that committee, this fund, that organisation. Someone who can be reasoned with and who shares their vision. In many cases, the person standing in for them is unaware of the power of their benefactors. They are looked upon as merely financial backers or connected individuals who use their wealth for social good and philanthropy. The masks are complex and do not slip. Too much is at stake. They dream of a new world order where unsanctioned war is a thing of the past. Peace, but on their terms.

Jack was absorbing everything and making notes in his own dossier. In fact, he was creating one for Clog and another for himself. Clog had no need to know everything. And Jack couldn't know everything. He could piece together scenes and conversations in the past, but the present was undocumented thus far.

"The only thing more powerful than finance is the industry it funds—if only for the moment. Industry creates wealth. Simply put, we can't win as long as they continue to prosper while simultaneously cutting our advances towards integration with the modern financial model. I don't know why they are being so stubborn. It's 2015, for Christ's sake." Herr Oberdorff pushed his yellow pad away from him as an expression of the finality of his statement.

The other ten members of the order sat silently. It was a moment before Madame Bettenfroid replied.

"Well gentlemen, what are our options?"

"As you know," started Mr. Clark, "we simply lack the influence in China and it will take us at least a decade to infiltrate the upper echelons. The top position is generally held for ten years or more and the current general secretary has a deep distrust of the West—despite superficial actions and rhetoric to the contrary."

"Can we not wait?" The voice was heavily accented. Despite decades of elocution, Mr. Franca was unable to choke his Italian accent. "Time is our ally in most things."

"Agreed, but we didn't anticipate the geometric growth combined with social cohesion currently being witnessed in China. If we don't act, our advantage will be lost and a century of effort wasted." The other American was leaning forward, face reddening despite his otherwise implacable demeanour.

"Do we have an alternative?" asked a voice. The conversation had stayed mainly between the Germans and Americans, but this voice was likely English or a refined Frenchman.

"Unfortunately, no," Mr. Rock conceded. His New York accent cut through the room. His voice had carried many an argument over the previous four decades and his lack of flexibility encouraged the radical elements within the group.

"Then perhaps we should take a more aggressive stance?" said the same voice. It was English. Mr. Roth. His family was a voice that had carried enormous weight for the last two centuries, but in recent times held less sway.

"Are you saying what I think you're saying?" Herr Oberdorff sputtered.

"We've done it before."

"But look at the troubles we had. And the repercussions are endless if not done properly."

"Then we need to do it properly."

There was silence.

"I move that we take a break and reconvene in thirty minutes. Hopefully we'll have a better idea of how to proceed." Mr. Rock was the voice of reason and everyone agreed.

Six weeks later, the general secretary was shot. The plan didn't go as they had hoped. The members of the order would need to wait until their day jobs brought them into contact with each other sometime soon. This usually meant a crisis talk over the state of the euro, or the regularly scheduled meetings of the G12, or perhaps the implosion of a region's economy that required urgent Western intervention. These members of the ultra-secretive Order of the Prime would ensure that they were invited to these global gatherings. No one would dream of not including them and they would be free to meet up and discuss their own plans, but always in secret.

∞

"Consumption is the key. If we can't evolve their economy into one of consumerism, we will see everything we worked for collapse. All of our efforts are pooling in the reserves of China's surpluses. Until we reverse that, we are vulnerable."

The members looked concerned. Not for themselves, as they each had more money than they could spend in a hundred lifetimes, but that the current path of China could unintentionally derail their plans. They had painstakingly laid the rails of finance for the world and now China was determined to go its own way.

"How do we alter the direction of one and a half billion people? If we can't stop them, perhaps we can direct them." Again, the voice of reason. Mr. Rock knew that a small stream could eventually divert a river, whereas a dam prematurely built would be pushed aside from the shear momentum of the water. So too with people and their finances. They just needed a way to penetrate the seemingly unstoppable torrent that was China's modernisation and slowly take control of its currency and financial policy. "This group achieved much more with much less a century ago. We need to determine whether we still have the stomach for this or whether we have done all we can."

The Order of the Prime was not infallible. Its members were not omniscient. They were just people, subject to weaknesses—greed, hate, lust—and every so often a member needed to be replaced. It usually started with a conversation such as this. Those who knew better kept quiet. Membership of this order was for life. A person was not asked lightly and they kept lists of potential candidates and monitored their reactions over decades. If anything in their past or present raised a concern, they were struck from consideration. The candidate would never even know they were being considered. The order couldn't allow their existence to become known. But the order didn't run the world. No one could run the world. They were merely trying to apply enlightened and rational thought to a chaotic and mad system. To that end, they realised that only capital wisely employed could achieve their desired aims.

The Dossier

Carey noticed the change in Jack's behaviour. It was subtle but there was a difference. From the first moment she met him, she liked the way he looked, walked and talked. He was handsome but not in a pretty way. Masculine but still vulnerable. It was the pain in his eyes that drew her to him the most. She wanted to protect him. And he allowed her to. In some ways, he was protecting her as well. But lately, there was a new look in his eyes, a more determined walk, and greater passion in bed. She wasn't complaining but she wanted to know why.

"Everything okay Jack?" she asked.

"Everything's great," he said. He was working on something on his computer, barely looking up.

"Anything important?"

"What?"

"Anything important that you're working on? You've been at it for weeks now. Sometimes I wonder if you even notice that I'm here."

Jack closed his computer and put it aside. "I notice you when you are in the same building as me. I feel you when you are in the same room as me. I can't stop touching you when you are next to me."

"Oooh, keep talking," she said. "I like it." She kissed him as she went to make some more coffee.

"Can you get me another refill as well? Thanks." Jack turned back to his computer and started working.

Carey couldn't help but look in his direction as the familiar sounds registered in her head. The click of the laptop opening and the keystrokes' muffled staccato filled the room. She put the coffee next to him and cuddled up. She liked her time with Jack. She had never known a man like him before. The only other man to have this effect on her was unavailable—no wife, just a job that prevented a relationship. She wondered at the difference her life trajectory would have taken if she stayed with that man. She'd still be in the UK, possibly working at the same firm as him.

"Who's Herr Oberdorff?" She couldn't help but see some of the names Jack was working on.

"Uh, just some guy who's part of an organisation I'm trying to understand."

"Work?"

"Kind of. I'm trying to piece together a puzzle with eleven components. I've found seven and still need to find the other four."

"Can I help?"

"Not really. I'd get fired over this if anyone found out you even saw this." Jack looked at Carey and shrugged, as if the gesture explained it better. He had a sip of coffee. "Thanks for the coffee."

"No problem. Look, I don't need to know and I don't want to know. I just noticed that you're working non-stop on whatever this is. If I can help, I will."

"Thanks," he said. Then, "there is something. I think I'm supposed to be going to London in the next few weeks. It would be amazing if you could join me."

"In a heartbeat," she said. Her heart did skip a beat as the thought of her ex drifted into her head. *Don't be so stupid,* she said to herself. *That's just a fantasy. You have reality in front of you.* Then, "what about the trouble with flying. Remember the problems we had just trying to go to Hawaii or Florida?"

"I think it's all taken care of. Some administrative error, apparently. I somehow got onto the no-fly list. My employer sorted that out for me. Otherwise, I wouldn't be going anywhere." Jack smiled sheepishly. It wasn't a total lie. "In that case," Carey said, "my answer is yes. I just need to clear it at work but I'm owed some holiday time. As long as the notice isn't too short I should be okay to go."

"Excellent. Sounds like a plan. Now all I need to do is find those other four bastards before we leave…"

∞

Primrose Hill, North London

Jack enjoyed his meal at Lemonia. It was a meze, a sort of tasting menu that allows the eater to enjoy the flavours and delicacies on offer. It was a Greek restaurant popular with the locals. It was loud with people laughing and talking, but it remained friendly and down to earth. Across from him sat a young man from China who appeared to be of similar age to himself. His name was Wang Wei and they were sitting in this particular restaurant because James and Denise insisted.

"How's the food?" Jack ventured.

"Very good, thanks. A bit loud, though." Wei was tall and athletic and all the plates on their table had been polished clean. He had obviously learned that, in the West, it was polite to finish all of the food if you liked it. In China, it would have been rude for him to have eaten everything.

"Do you want to continue our conversation outside? It doesn't seem to be raining and I wouldn't mind walking off some of this meal." Jack was staying on the other side of the hill where the roads intersected, giving him good subway access as well as taxis and green space to walk and feel human.

Wei paused, thinking about the consequences. He was a very thoughtful and cautious man, Jack noticed.

"Sounds good. I'll get the bill." Wei had the mannerisms and language down pat. He was polite, cautious, and reflective. He even kept his job after the assassination attempt on his boss. He was one of the favoured and had a future among the power brokers and wielders of China's difficult and treacherous political system.

They got up and levered their chairs to slide past the neighbouring tables. They each wore the expected suits of the professional class. Jack's was purchased in Harrods at the last minute with Carey (who managed to get some time off work and had joined him). It was all of one day old.

Remember that in the real world, you are judged by the way you look. We'll get you the best shoes from Church's, a superb Italian suit from Harrods, and the best crisp white shirt you've ever seen. Jack could hear the voices of his handlers. They made such a big deal of the little details. Carey bought him a beautiful silk tie from some fancy designer. He would cherish that more than everything else.

Perhaps the saying was true: the clothes make the man. Shakespeare, naturally, said it better: "...the apparel oft proclaims the man." *It's one thing for me to put on a costume but quite another for that costume to transform me into the class of the clothes,* Jack thought. *I'm no super-agent, regardless of the clothes.* Do the right shoes make you jump higher, run faster, and look cooler? Cooler, possibly, but the other traits are an example of how consumerism has trained us. Jack had come to realise that while clothes didn't make you, the wrong clothes could break you.

They walked along the pavement towards Regents Park. It was a pleasant walk and the weather was cooperative. It hadn't rained in a couple of days and the ground was dry. The summer evening still had enough light and the parks were full of couples sitting around, friends throwing Frisbees and kicking footballs, and mothers pushing their prams. Dog walkers preferred this time of day and the dogs, for the most part, were well behaved.

"Thanks for that," Jack said, nodding his head towards the restaurant.

"No problem. Expense account." Wei smiled.

Jack walked in silence for a few moments before he broached the subject. "Do you have any idea why we're supposed to talk?"

"Not really. I was told you have some information that would be invaluable and help find the culprits behind the assassination attempt." His pronunciation failed him in the quiet evening air. In the restaurant, Jack was struck by how well he spoke. Now he could hear the tell-tale accents of the foreigner, especially in multisyllabic words. Wei was fluent and understandable, but it was not native.

"I think we do but I need to be careful. We both need to be careful." It was conspiratorial.

"What do you need from me to help you deliver this information?"

"I need assurances this will be told to your boss and that it will be actioned." Jack sounded like a seasoned agent but was, in fact, perspiring greatly. His parents coached him and he vowed to do his best. He was in the deep end of the pool. Sink or swim time.

"Of course."

"It's dangerous."

Wei laughed. "How much more dangerous can it be? He has already almost died."

"Dangerous to you. And me." James' words echoed in Jack's head.

Wei became serious again. "Look, you obviously feel you have something very important and I would be happy to work with you to get this information out."

Jack interrupted him. "Not just important information. If I am correct, this affects your entire government and way of life." Jack became irritable at himself and decided he had messed up the entire mission. "Look, it was great meeting you and I hope we can stay in touch. Let me talk things over with my people and I'll get back to you. Is there any way I can get in touch with you securely?"

Wei stopped walking and turned to Jack. Jack was sweating more visibly and Wei could see he was uncomfortable. He put out his hand. "I'll be in touch with you, Jack. At that point, we can establish if and how we stay in touch."

Jack smiled. Wei was much better at this than he was. He shook his hand and Wei flagged down a taxi.

Jack watched the car disappear and started walking again.

∞

"How'd your meeting go?" The voice was music to Jack's ears.

"Not bad. I'll know more in the next few days." He kicked off his shoes and removed his suit jacket.

Carey liked him like this. He looked powerful in his crisp white shirt, athletic body, and gorgeous tie. He was a cool guy but he really didn't have a clue when it came to men's fashion. She was in loose pyjamas and sitting cross legged in the middle of their hotel bed. She liked being back in London. Their hotel wasn't too far from where she went to school.

Carey's parents were hippies in the sixties. Her mother grew up to become a conventional stay-at-home housewife and her father became a civil servant who worked for the grain commission. Her father's job sounded boring but it meant that they were stationed in London during her teen years and Kenya during her formative years. It wasn't as dramatic as some military families but the results were similar: she made friends easily and didn't form attachments.

During a rebellious phase of her late teens, she met an older man named Edward. He dressed smart, had impeccable manners, and opened doors for her she couldn't have imagined. She tried to join him after her schooling in the UK but his employer said no. They stayed in touch but he made an indelible impression on her. She had vowed to try again with him if she ever found herself in the UK.

"Can I do anything to help?"

Jack smiled. "Not with my work, but I do have an idea of what you can do for me." He took off his tie and started walking towards the bed.

"I wonder what that might be."

"We'll just have to play that one by ear." Jack was down to his boxers and slid next to Carey. He enjoyed her body next to his. He kissed her on her neck, between her shoulder and ear. She moved her head towards him as he kissed her, shoulder rising as if a bit ticklish.

"By the way," she said as his hands started feeling her through her clothes, "I have an appointment tomorrow in the city. I hope that's okay with your schedule."

Jack didn't reply. He murmured something, but his mind was elsewhere.

∞

The next day, Jack hung around the hotel while Carey went for her appointment. She didn't go to the City, and instead went to a well-known address near Lambeth Bridge, off Millbank. Number 12 Millbank. MI5's headquarters.

Carey had wanted to join the MI5 shortly after completing her International Baccalaureate at the American School of London. Since she wasn't British, that was a non-starter, but she did become friendly with an agent and had stayed in touch.

"Aren't you a sight for sore eyes," Edward said as he kissed her on each cheek. He held onto her arms a little longer and looked at her. *She's still a stunner*, he thought.

"Hi Ed. Thanks for seeing me. You don't mind that I came down, do you?"

"No, not at all. It has been a long time, though, and I did wonder what I've done to deserve your attention…" He smiled. He was hoping she would flirt back and possibly reignite their relationship. He regretted MI5's decision to not make her an agent, but he managed to maintain her as an asset.

"I don't have too long, but I thought you might be interested in something that I came across. I don't know all of the details."

Ed forgot about bedding Carey and refocussed. "What are you trying to tell me?"

"I think something big is happening and I wanted you to know about it. You'll know what to do more than I will."

"Sounds ominous. What is it?"

"Not totally certain, but it involves China and the US and the most recent assassination attempt on the secretary general."

Ed let out a low whistle. "Good stuff, but above my pay grade I'm afraid. I'll need to get someone more senior."

"Okay, but I don't have anything specific just yet. I just wanted to give you a heads up and perhaps establish a way for me to give you information in the future without me physically coming here."

"Understood. Follow me. I'll let the IT guys give you the details."

Carey didn't feel any guilt as she followed Ed, and that concerned her a little. It also reinforced that she was doing the right thing.

∞

"In 1933, the US dollar devalued 70% against gold. As all reserve currencies were backed by gold, it was essential for governments to agree what their currency was worth from time to time. In the past, a century could pass without any significant devaluation of Sterling or the dollar. But the consequences of WWI created a different type of war, one between the currencies of Europe." Jack was looking at Wei as he spoke, searching for recognition and understanding. They had met in the Starbucks near the Chinese embassy.

"Okay," Wei said. "And?" He was cautious and retained his wariness of the West.

"The next major event was between 1971 and 1980—nearly a 95% devaluation." Jack was speaking slowly, trying to mentally tick the points that his parents' dossier set out.

"I remember studying that period. I don't remember that level of devaluation."

"I'm talking about devaluation against a fixed item: gold. In relative terms, the dollar has gone down against the other global currencies, but that was engineered. The dollar was then acting as the anchor for the world's currencies."

Wei was listening and trying to see where the conversation was heading. He couldn't see how this had anything to do with the assassination attempt against his boss.

"Recently, from 2008-2017, we saw a further devaluation of 50% or more against gold. When the financial crisis struck, there was only one option in the playbook: devaluation by any and all means. Print money, fictionalise the creation of new money's effect on the value of existing money, and drop interest rates."

"But how is this relevant to our last discussion?"

"I'll get there, but I wanted to set the scene first. In 1930, there were effectively two global reserve currencies—the English Pound Sterling and the US Dollar. But both were backed by gold, so there was little risk for those who used those reserve currencies. In 1945, there was only one global reserve currency, the US dollar—again, backed by gold. But then things changed. The pressures against the world's currencies no longer made it easy for a currency to be backed by gold. A gold-backed currency required overt devaluation and everyone would see the result of the inflation and devaluation on their wealth. To overcome this, the US dollar broke with the gold standard in 1971. Over the next decade, the dollar plummeted against gold but eventually stabilised against all of the other global currencies. The dollar survived the transition and became the global anchor."

Wei was listening but was growing less patient.

"Over the next forty years, the US dollar reigned supreme, but it was still vulnerable. It wasn't practical for one country to effectively dictate monetary policy to the world now that physical war had passed. Europe combined into the euro, which is flawed in its current state. It is a rival and credible global reserve currency to the dollar, but we also see the rise of the Yuan or Renminbi of China. It too has claims to be a global reserve currency."

With mention of the Renminbi, Wei's ears perked up. But he was still struggling with how any of this was relevant. "Okay, but who cares? I'm not an economist and this stuff is handled by the world's experts in that field. And how does this relate to the assassination attempt?"

"They're all linked. There is a group that has been promoting and guiding the global financial community towards a global currency without ties to any country and strong enough to be independent of any metal such as gold and flexible enough to respond at the touch of a button—a button controlled by them. These same people didn't like the path that your boss was on and decided to remove him."

Wang Wei was silent. "It all sounds a bit far-fetched, don't you think? All too much of a conspiracy and too easy of an explanation. The world is a complicated place with infinite movements. It's impossible for a handful of people to control so many moving parts."

"But a handful of people run China. And a handful of people run Canada, run Russia, run the US, run France, run anywhere. These are ostensibly the elected politicians with the secretary general or prime minister or president at the top. They run the country." Jack paused for effect. "But we both know there are people behind the throne who pull certain strings. They are the operators and financiers who get the politicians elected. They don't care what day your garbage is collected or whether school children are bussed. At the very highest levels, these financiers' interests include the creation of a global currency outside the hands of the elected politicians or even of nations themselves."

Wei listened. He was starting to see what Jack was saying but it still was too muddy.

Jack continued. "Your boss is likely to be in power for at least ten years, maybe more. His policies do not coincide with this group. Simple as that. China is too large to be ignored or allowed to go its own way. This was simply a crude attempt to bring about a prompt solution. It is likely they have become impatient. They operate in decades, not days, so this is uncharacteristic." Jack paused as an idea entered his mind. "Perhaps they were impatient because they have already set things in motion."

"How certain are you?" Wei asked.

"Everything is public knowledge. Everything except the group, which has taken some research. Very certain." Jack was feeling good about himself. All these years of studying finance gave him a firm grip on the subject. But he also had sight of highly confidential CIA documents backing up his theories. Now he needed to get Wei to see the light.

"Okay, but apart from killing people—which seems a bit extreme and highly unlikely—what is the harm in creating a global currency? It sounds like it may even be a good thing. No exchange issues when travelling, everyone knows where they stand. Why fight this?"

Jack stopped. He had wondered the same thing. Who cares who pulls the strings? Someone always will be. "I agree that it's not very high on people's lists of concerns. Definitely not up there with global warming and probably even lower than whether or not to take your shoes off when you visit a stranger's home. But let me put it another way: What's your favourite game?"

"I like go, but not many people play it outside of Asia. I like chess too, if that helps."

"Perfect. When you play chess, you have an agreed set of rules. The rules are independent of the game. Both players are subject to the same restrictions and advantages. But say one player is able to dictate the rules of the game as he sees fit. As you sit down, he decides that your players must conform to conventional movements—for example, pawns can advance up to two squares on the first move, once thereafter, and capture by going diagonally. But while you are constrained to the conventional rules, he decides that his pawns all have the power of queens—in other words, each of his lowest value pieces have the same value as your highest value piece. Do you think you would have a fair game?"

Wei looked at Jack until he realised it wasn't a rhetorical question. "No, of course not," he said.

"After you played once, would you want to play against him under those circumstances again?"

"No. It ceases to be a game if the rules are not applied equally between both parties. The game is rigged."

"Exactly. Games should be about skill and luck, just like life. Games hone skills for life but we play them because they're fun. We can play, replay, and learn from games."

Wei was silent. He didn't get it.

"If we have a global currency controlled by a handful of people, there is the real probability that they will skew its value. It's a moral hazard and if there is one thing you can be sure of, it's that people will eventually succumb to temptation. We live in a world so finely tuned that even the slightest manipulation reverberates throughout the fabric of the world's financial systems."

Wei was seeing the point. "And if they are able to manipulate the lifeblood of nations," he said, "the power of keeping peace, waging war, and everything in between becomes subject to their consideration." He started gaining momentum as the magnitude of such a seemingly simple idea took hold. "New hospitals? What policy do I want to follow—preferably one that reflects the people of the nation? We have seen that Greece does not run itself culturally like the Germans. The Russians operate and prioritise differently than the Chinese. The Americans and Mexicans live next to each other but they are worlds apart. I can see your point. Whoever controls the money controls the nation."

Jack was pleased. "To quote from one of my favourite movies: 'Finance is the gun, politics is knowing when to pull the trigger.' If that is true, then the creation of the global currency would be tantamount to loss of sovereignty."

"They would take over the world without a shot being fired—other than manufactured wars to protect the currency of the day." Wei reluctantly agreed with Jack that the Iraq war could have been more about protecting the supremacy of the dollar than oil. "What can be done?" asked Wei. "We are only a couple of insects on the back of an elephant. This seems to be something that has been set in motion decades ago and has real momentum."

"Yes, we are nobodies," said Jack. "But your boss is a somebody. A big somebody. He has the power to thwart these plans."

"If he believes me. He has a mind of his own and the Chinese people are complicated. No one man decides anything."

"That's all we can hope for."

"But what is the solution?"

"I don't know. All I do know is that if people truly understood the facts, they wouldn't wish to put themselves in a position to lose control over their own destiny. This group has proven that it will kill to enforce its will and put the blood on the hands of everyone but themselves. More recently, we have seen that they are also willing to get their own hands dirty."

Both of their coffees had gone cold. They didn't notice. They were both in their own worlds. Jack was glad to have met Wei and Wei was trying to determine whether this was all a bunch of crazy talk. He couldn't appear to be reckless or reactive when talking to his boss.

They agreed to stay in touch and shook hands.

Wei left to return to his embassy, while Jack ordered a fresh coffee to go. He would walk back to his hotel room. He was too wound up to sit still.

Neither Wei nor Jack noticed a well-dressed Englishman sitting two tables over, his back to them. He had been listening without looking like he was. The pages of his newspaper periodically turned, giving the impression of him reading. He had been drinking a hot chocolate and was slowly eating a Danish pastry. He looked like any other suited businessmen taking a break from their day.

As Jack walked out, that same businessman made some notes on his pad and tapped out a text to his boss. "We need to meet." *Carey really came through on this one,* thought Ed to himself. He folded his paper and left it for the next customer.

Chapter Eleven

History Repeated

Jack's meeting with Wei was encouraging and he was working hard to identify the last members of the secretive group. What he discovered was a pattern of control and leadership at the very top. Two families had representatives on the group for over 140 years. And one family had been a driving force within the group since its origins. In fact, this same family was a force in its predecessor, the Illuminati.

Jack realised he needed to dig deeper and understand the histories of both the Roths and Rocks. And to do that, he needed to dig until he found the very beginning of their stories.

∞

Roth

"When they come, you need to drop everything and run." Amschel looked intently at his son. "And when you are on the run, you will need to have the ability to stay alive. To stay alive, you need skills."

Amschel was not well and would be lucky if he lived to see the Jewish New Year, Rosh Hashanah. He was dying of smallpox and was not yet forty-five years old. His favourite son, Mayer, was nearly twelve years old. Amschel had initially wanted his son to become a Rabbi and be a good Jew. It was 1755 and they lived in the most liberal of cities for Jews—Frankfurt, Germany. They were allowed property provided they stayed away from the Christians and didn't go out or mingle outside of their ghetto during Christian holidays.

"I have arranged a position in court for you, my son," Amschel continued. "Be a good boy and study hard and distinguish yourself. I have had the honour to make the acquaintance of the prince and I have a good name there. You will carry the name of Roth proudly in all that you do. Remember that your word and your mind are all you have in this world. They are your currency on which you will trade and make your way."

Mayer kneeled dutifully next to his father's bed and was silent. He was already a man at twelve and would both study and work hard. He had a head for numbers and a good memory for people's faces and stories. He had accompanied his father during his trips trading silk and trading coins. He understood the different values that people gave to money and coins. This gave him a different outlook than many older man, and his talent would be disguising his adult understanding in his boy's body.

Amschel blessed his son and said a prayer as Mayer knelt. It was a quiet room with just a small square window in the corner. The bed was low and covered with the best that they could afford. Next to the bed lay a volume of the Mishna, the codified tradition of Judaism as presented to Moses and the Children of God as they wandered in the desert and beyond. God's word and the high priests' interpretations thereof was passed from generation to generation orally until shortly after the second destruction of the temple in Jerusalem by the Romans. At that point, Judaism faced a crisis of existence. It was determined that the oral traditions would be written down. Many disagreed and their interpretations of the word of God have been silenced over time through death and dispersion. The written word survived and Amschel would comfort himself in its wisdom on all things. It was sometimes referred to as the oral Torah. Christians read the words of Moses, as did the Jews. These were the first five books of the Christian Old Testament, attributed to Moses and called the Pentateuch. The Jews held those same books to be especially sacred and called it the Torah. That day, Amschel started from the beginning again and reached for the Torah, ignoring the Mishna. Genesis. No place like the beginning—especially as Amschel's own end was so near.

Amschel knew how fragile their safety and relative prosperity was. Germany was one of the few enlightened countries where a person could study and practice his religion without persecution. He heard stories of the pogroms of the various countries in Europe; he knew people who personally suffered terrible assaults purely because they held different beliefs than their neighbours. But Amschel also knew that this same intolerance existed between Christians. Killings, burnings and massacres were conducted in the name of their Christ. Christianity was a religion of love and forgiveness, but Amschel couldn't see it. He only saw their hate and fear. He was thankful that he and his family lived in Germany. He knew no harm would ever come to him or his people from the Germans.

Amschel had contacts at court. He had a home and all of his extended family lived there. When he died, he hoped that Mayer would be able to leverage his contacts. Amschel needed to believe that he had been successful in bettering his family's lives.

Little did he imagine the power and prestige Mayer would generate. It took another generation after Mayer, but by then the Roths became the richest and most powerful family on the planet. Kings bestowed titles to their descendants and people would speak their name in hushed tones. Mayer distilled all of the wisdom of his people and was determined to stop running. He knew that once you go on the run, there was nowhere to hide and no one to turn to. His father's dying words warned him of what was engrained as inevitable. He was determined to make that inevitability someone else's problem.

Mayer apprenticed at a well-known banking firm famed for lending to royalty and operated by court Jews. He learned the ins and outs of court and banking and distinguished himself. In 1769, only fourteen years after that conversation with his father, the prince himself granted Mayer the power to collect taxes on his behalf and to supervise his extensive holdings. At the time, the prince was among the wealthiest men in all of Europe, but would shortly become richest of them all. Mayer was barely twenty-six years old. During all of this time, Mayer continued his father's trading business with an eye to creating his own bank someday.

The prince came to trust Mayer absolutely. So great was his trust that when, decades later, the prince needed to hide money from the French during the Napoleonic wars, he chose Mayer Roth's Frankfurt offices. As luck and foresight would have it, Mayer's son was stationed in England and much of those monies from the prince found their way there. Mayer's son was then in a position to fund England's war against France, with such effect that the Roths' bank was credited with saving England. Naturally, the prince was not credited himself, but he received his money back when it was safe again. He was grateful for the security and discretion exercised by his Jewish friends.

Mayer had foreseen the power of information and position. He had five sons stationed in Europe's major capitals. He believed in family, trust, and dedication. He had played his role as a father and founder of a real business and had trained his sons well. No son of his would feel the fear of running.

Soon the Illuminati made contact with Mayer. This secretive order, of which the prince was already a member, helped secure the sense of trust that enabled the prince to place his gold and wealth at Mayer's disposal. It was this order and its successor that future Roths would preside over and ensure an inside perspective of the world's events.

∞

Back in the twenty-first century, Mr. Roth mused about his forefathers' daring and foresight. Without the prince and his contacts, the House of Roth would have been prosperous, but not at the levels achieved in such a short period. He grimaced at his English ancestor's words shortly after saving the kingdom:

I care not what puppet is placed upon the throne of England to rule the Empire on which the sun never sets. The man who controls Britain's money supply controls the British Empire, and I control the British money supply.

It was foolish and vane and would be quoted endlessly by conspiracy theorists who couldn't understand how some immigrants could have so thoroughly dominated their homeland.

Mr. Roth thought of the endless numbers of migrants on the nightly news and television, fleeing war zones and famine, searching for a safe place to lay their heads and raise their families. He thought of the horrors of World War II and the way the world turned its back on the Jews of Germany. He thought of how unthinkable it was for Germany to turn on its own people. So much had happened to so many people. How was it that he and his family survived, even prospered, while so many others suffered? It was the answer to this that drove him towards his family's long-standing goal of a global currency with central control by the enlightened few. Peace was achieved and war was fought with gold and currency. Take this away and there would be no war. Supply it correctly and there would be peace. Starve the fire of oxygen and it goes out. It was simple but true. His English ancestor may have been imprudent in his choice of words, but their truth was as real today as it was two hundred years ago.

It matters not what puppet is placed in the White House or in any of the corridors of power in the world. Those who control the world's money supply control the world—and we will control the world's money supply. Mr. Roth smiled as he paraphrased his ancestor's words. The question was, who would sit alongside him at this seat of ultimate power? And would he need to share that seat at all?

∞

Rock

"Thank you ma'am. You have just saved your own life. That tincture, if taken correctly, will help you sleep better and keep any cancers from developing in your body."

"Thank you, Dr. Levingston, and God bless you. You truly are one of God's creatures." Mrs. Smith held the folded bag with her left hand and shook Dr. Levingston's hand. She was fifty-six years old and living on her own in upstate New York. She came to meet the travelling doctor after seeing pamphlets about his miracle cure stapled on the notice board at her church.

"You are too kind, Mrs. Smith," replied the doctor. "Remember, it's already 1849 and soon there will be no disease in this world. All people need to do is to listen to nature and be healed by the natural medicine found in the grasses, roots, and berries all around us. God bless you and don't forget to write for more of your medicine if you want it to work." With that, he closed the side panel to his cart and walked to his horse.

Dr. Levingston wasn't a doctor. His name wasn't even Levingston. It was Rock. He tried to make money any way he could but found it difficult. He tried forestry and lumber sales and any number of get rich schemes, but they all failed for one reason or another. His current persona was that of a travelling botanist, a doctor who had found the cure for cancer and any other disease you could name. He was a fraud, a womaniser, and a bigamist. He was also the great-great-grandfather of the Mr. Rock who sat amongst the most powerful men and women in the world in the opening years of the twenty-first century.

This rogue left the patriarch and founder of one of the greatest family dynasties of the western world when the boy was barely sixteen years old. This boy grew up in modest circumstances, mindful of his god, and had two life objectives: to earn $100,000 and to live to be a hundred years old. He started as an assistant bookkeeper to a fruit and vegetable producer. He loved every minute of the hard and meticulous work. Within a few years, he opened his own firm and made money every year. Then, spotting a new technology in oil, he found some partners and created one of the first oil refineries in 1863. He worked hard and was adamant that he should give at least ten percent of everything he earned to charity. As part of this lifelong habit of saving and frugality, he was able to buy out his partners in 1865 and began borrowing heavily. He invested every penny and worked continuously. At his peak, Rock Senior, as he was known, controlled 90% of the oil industry and sought to form a monopoly in everything he touched. He was an industrialist of the highest order with power that protected him from almost everything.

In 1880, Rock Senior was invited into the Order of the Prime. Shortly thereafter, he was to meet Mr. Roth and together they sought to form the greatest monopoly the world would have ever known—if the world ever heard about it (and they had no intention of advertising this monopoly). Rock and Roth pulled the strings of those who controlled those in power. They learned to wield power twice and thrice removed from the public. They preferred the privacy of anonymity, although that was a difficult task considering their public personas.

One of the greatest coups engineered by Rock and Roth was the great trust busting legislation initiated by the US government, ostensibly aimed at dissipating the power held by the few to distribute it into the hands of the many. The outward result was the breakup of Rock's publicly known holdings, which received great fanfare. The real result was an even more obscene amount of wealth and power accumulated by Rock as each arm of his former titanic company became a heavyweight in its own right, buoyed by public valuations and participation. All he needed to do was sit tight and focus on his distractions, as he called them—his participation in the Order of the Prime and its objective of making the world a better place.

Between them at their height of power, Roth and Rock owned just over 1% of the world's wealth, but they controlled over 15% and influenced almost 40%. When their influence waned, they put in place a strategy for future generations to maintain a say in world events. Out of obscurity and poverty, these two giants of finance and industry bestrode the world and did their utmost to influence everyone to their thinking and objectives. By the time the current Mr. Roth and Mr. Rock were in charge, a plan was established for the creation of a global currency. It was a long time in the making but both dynasties knew the power of structural control of a country's finances and resources. The new global currency represented an impossibly complex system of new money that Roth and Rock would dominate and others would be incapable of replicating. It was similar to Roth's ancestors' tactics in funding England to defeat France's Napoleon with the prince's gold.

∞

Jack was able to fill in some of the gaps from history books. The CIA dossiers simply clarified which lens he needed to view his subjects. Knowing their destination and mind-set allowed him to recreate their true histories as it related to their obsession with a global currency.

From what he could discover, the obsession began from an off-hand remark where one member wished they could simply create gold. Another was complaining at the difficulty of creating wealth and the time it took to affect their strategies. Everything would be easier with a currency they could control. They started with the creation of central banks and moved progressively towards a currency disconnected from gold and even nations.

∞

Mr. Rock was furious. He was getting on in age and he wished there was another member with his vigour prepared to lead the group. Despite having such enormous power and influence, the group's members acted like a fraternity with a sense of entitlement and laziness. They acted seriously and made all the right sounds, but they were fundamentally cowards. Many of them just liked being part of the group. An idea began to form in Rock's mind.

"We need to be cautious," Herr Oberdorff pleaded. "Our actions were reckless and we are now facing the consequences. It's dangerous to proceed."

"What was reckless?" interjected Madame Bettenfroid. "Our actions in China recently or our inactions these last decades?"

"You know what I mean," said Oberdorff. "We were reckless in advancing the SDRs without properly preparing the groundwork. The branding of the project, if you will."

It was Mr. Franca's time to speak. "Operation GC was well prepared and it was a success in 1969 and throughout the seventies. It was successful and well received in the latest crisis of '09. We now have over a quarter of a trillion dollars in SDRs and a number of Nobel Prize winners talking about our plan without us even promoting it. I disagree. We are right on track and right on time."

"Agreed," said Clark. "We need to implement the humanitarian element of our plan immediately. It will allow us to increase the amount of SDRs into the trillions with little pushback from the rest of the world. The press will hail the idea as a victory of smart capital over poverty. And then we need only wait."

"I agree with Mr. Clark," said Mr. Rock. None of them ever referred to each other by their first names. "Let's push forward with our aid to developing nations. We can, in one stroke, eliminate all of their debt and free the impoverished people from their current financial burdens." He didn't bother to explain that these countries' new debts would be just as crippling, but that was all part of the beauty of the system. "All we need to do is to issue enough SDRs to these countries, possibly in the region of $300 billion worth per year, given to them pro rata with their needs and population. These countries could then deposit the monies with the IMF to fund the national needs. The math has already been done. We had the IMF publish a road map for this back in 2011. Despite all of our efforts, SDR's current capacity is only at just under $600 billion globally. We need to increase that number dramatically and in a way that will receive support internationally. The humanitarian angle is the way to go."

"It would be the greatest transfer of wealth at the same time as the greatest creation of wealth in human history," purred Madame Bettenfroid. "Being able to simply give away $300 billion per year is an astounding amount of money. And knowing it will simply come back to us, I mean the IMF, would give security for the entire project. I am proud of this order and I am proud of all we have accomplished so far. Thanks to each and every one of you. It is a shame that all of our good work will never be acknowledged."

"Hear hear," said Mr. Roth.

The other members of the order rarely talked. They listened, they commented quietly, but rarely butted heads with the alphas. They too beamed with pride at the historic juncture they had reached. They were on the edge of eliminating poverty. Surely, that trumped other considerations?

∞

Jack had created an entire dossier simply on SDRs. SDRs were Special Drawing Rights, but there was nothing magical about them. They drew upon a basket of currencies instead of gold or any single currency. The system was used during times of monetary distress and introduced by the IMF in 1969. It wasn't utilised much at first, but the order wanted it to be in place to establish some heritage and provenance to its branded currency. He had learned that it was code-named (unimaginatively) Operation GC—which stood for the new global currency initiative.

In 2009, the order was able to push the G20 to use the IMF's instrument to create $289 billion. This momentous use of SDRs went virtually unnoticed because of the even more distressing global financial meltdown facing the public at the time. The order tried to establish a toe-hold for their favoured instrument, with the G20 and IMF as their preferred public-facing political bodies. *It was a concerted and unabashed attempt at unseating the dollar as the global reserve currency,* Jack thought. They were impatient and reckless. They misjudged the level of toxicity in the financial veins of Europe and the US, and that contagion poisoned their launch. Jack realised that they merely retreated and had begun their wait for the next opportunity.

When China's financial might became clearer, the order decided that the elected general secretary of China could derail their plans, which had spanned generations. That was their next reckless action. Jack ensured that he carefully notated this for Wei. His only hope was for Wei to take this to his boss and for something to be done about it.

Chapter Twelve

Cleaning House

Jack had returned to the States. Carey, for some reason, decided to stay behind. It was uncharacteristic of her, but he trusted her. She wanted to visit with some of her friends and explore some opportunities for possibly working in the UK. Jack was easy going and figured that he could work anywhere. He would join her in the UK if she decided that was the preferred option.

"Hello, detective," said Jack. They were back in the same coffee shop where he first told Clog about his parents and the China connection.

"Hi, Jack," said Clog. He sipped his coffee. He didn't know what they did to the coffee here but it really was exceptional. "How was your trip?"

"Interesting," said Jack. "I met with the Chinese contact and told him everything my parents said. I have prepared a summary of my contact and our conversations. I think he will stay in touch with me. I have taken the liberty of using the same encrypted site we use to contact him." Jack paused, waiting to see if he had screwed up.

Clog looked uninterested so Jack continued.

"I just wanted to see if there is anything else you need from me. I don't think my parents can be of any more use."

Clog put his coffee down and looked at Jack. "You do realise you'll always be reporting to me, don't you?" He said it in such a matter of fact manner that Jack became crestfallen. He had hoped this was a one-off deal, that his help would buy him his freedom. He had assumed that Clog's bravado was just talk. He never thought he meant it.

"But that wasn't the deal I understood," said Jack.

"I can't help it if you're a bit slow."

Silence.

"Okay, so I'm dumb. What do I do now?"

"Go back to your job. I made sure it would still be there when you returned. Keep your ears to the ground and let me know if anything develops."

Jack, realising the conversation was over, got up and left the café. *I'll never be free*, he thought.

∞

The killing of one person really was not a big deal. The consequences of an unsanctioned kill could be unpleasant and eternal damnation was rarely a consideration for the assassin. Anyone could be killed, provided sufficient intelligence had been gathered. This is why most assassinations of top political figures invariably involved inside information.

But this wasn't an inside job.

It had taken almost six months of painstaking intelligence gathering before Jack's dossier containing eleven names were handed to Mary Rodriguez. She was thirty-four years old with glossy black straight hair and ice blue eyes. A product of many nationalities, her father was Icelandic-Czech and her mother was Mexican. It drove the men and a lot of women crazy to see her. She looked equally smashing in a tailored suit or skimpy bikini. Her hair looked so healthy that women would start up conversations with her to find out her secret. Men were hypnotised by her eyes. Her walk was confident, defiant and unstoppable.

She was a naturalised American and had served in the US Marines. The US Marines had enlisted woman as early as 1918 but women were never given duties that required them to be on the front line or receive equivalent training. While it has only been in the last couple of decades that women could receive combat training, Mary was singled out early for something else. As the marines didn't allow women into combat roles, there was no chance of her being trained as a sniper through them. Instead, in a highly unorthodox move, Mary was put into the Air Forces' sniping school. Records show that she didn't graduate and was drummed out.

In fact, she became an off the books operator for the government. Sometimes, a woman's touch was just what the military needed.

∞

Tuscany, Italy

Franca was enjoying the late autumn Tuscan sun and the new wine of the season. It was a fresh vintage and hadn't even been bottled. It still had a hint of continued fermentation. It was the wine enjoyed by peasants and nobility alike. Fresh, local, and different.

Franca had never earned anything in his life. It was all given to him. He was a third generation playboy industrialist. His family owned or was involved in everything from manufacturing of cars to electrical generation and infrastructure. As a young man, he prized his chiselled belly more than his bank account. He grew his hair long and spent most summers on the beach or on the family yacht. He received a decent education but was more interested in the extra-curricular events associated with university. Expensive, tight clothes highlighted his athletic frame. Even today, he wore his clothing a bit too tight and still saw himself as a young man instead of the old body in the mirror.

Over the years, Franca began to question the underlying philosophy he had chosen to adopt. In most things in life, you try before you buy. As his friends would always remind him: "If it flies, floats, or fucks, rent." Why he joined the order still puzzled him. He was a believer in what they aspired to, yes. He profited greatly from the association, yes. But it was how he was approached that sealed the deal.

Cardinal Benedict himself visited him to request that he, Franca, meet two distinguished guests. Franca knew of these two but never directly. Mr. Rock and Mr. Roth were those guests. After the pleasantries and evening dining was dispensed with, the three retired into the cardinal's private study. He was invited there and then. How could he say no?

And so he became one of the prime. But unlike planes, boats, or girlfriends, you couldn't try before you buy. You were in. And exiting was via the eternal pearly gates of Heaven.

Franca could live with this. It was the burden of leadership and power. Sometimes, responsibility came with unwanted consequences. One such burden was living with the stupid decisions occasionally made by the order, such as attempting an assassination on China's general secretary. That was almost a year ago now and becoming a distant memory.

Today, however, was not one of those days to regret. It was just before mid-day when he would sit down with his close friends for a two hour lunch followed by an afternoon snooze. He was hoping to share that snooze with the beauty he had met earlier that week. She was stunning. Glossy black hair and a body that was meant to wear a bikini. Smart, not smutty and proud. If she was a man, he would say she reminded him of himself when he was young.

∞

London, UK

Ed sat unobtrusively amidst the throngs at the Camden Lock Market. He couldn't help but chuckle to himself at tourists. How did this shithole become a top five destination for people visiting London?

He focussed on what he needed to achieve. A Nigerian diplomat's son had been approached by his colleagues to provide crucial feedback on the state of the inner machinations not yet cracked by the security services. The son was an intelligent young man studying at the London School of Economics. If the past was anything to go by, this asset would end up in a high position in future administrations within his country. It was all part of a new approach—long term grooming and early impact.

Ed saw Ojomola Adeleke make his way through the crowds towards a stall selling doughnuts and coffee. Even Ed had to admit that the doughnuts were first class. Ojomola was standing in line when he started talking to someone.

"You talking to me?" Ojo asked.

"Yeah, sorry. You look so happy and most people here are so miserable. I just thought…" She paused and wiped her palm against her pant leg and offered her hand. "Hi, I'm Carey."

"Hi, Ojo. Nice to meet you." Ojomola was a little awkward. He noticed that Carey didn't wear much make up at all, only a lip liner and a little something around the eyes. Her face dimpled when smiling and was round and friendly. He felt a jolt as he looked into her eyes. They looked at him as though she was looking at his soul.

"What was the question?" He felt a little foolish now.

"You look happy," Carey smiled. She knew this response. So far, so good.

Meanwhile, Ed noted contact and smiled again to himself. *She's good*, he thought. *These guys all had the same reaction to her. They never suspected.* Finally, she was part of his team officially and not just an asset being worked in the field.

∞

Paris, France

Bettenfroid looked at the timepiece on the credenza. It was an exquisite seventeenth century masterpiece by Thomas Tompion. But it was a gentleman's pocket watch and she was wary of its display. It required winding and while she paid to run the household, she didn't trust the staff completely (nor anyone else for that matter). She turned her left wrist and saw the time on her Cartier. It was French, of course. It wasn't the best watch nor the most expensive by far, but they made the best jewellery watches. She had five more minutes before she had to brave the crowds.

Generally, she enjoyed these events. All the great and good from around the world. Everyone was careful to not talk business, while at the same time bursting to be asked about anything that could lead to a pitch. Young beautiful women fluttered around, with whom she would swap lives in an instant—as long as she still had enough money to enjoy herself. Ah, youth; it truly was wasted on the young.

She emerged at ten minutes past the appointed time wearing a simple diamond necklace (of 153 carats) with a forty carat Burmese ruby hanging just at the right position on her chest. Simplicity was always best, she felt. On her finger she tended to wear the latest rage—presently, coloured diamonds. Today, she didn't. It clashed with the massive ruby hanging around her neck and however hard she tried, it looked garish to add colour to her fingers. Instead, she wore a bracelet of white sparkly diamonds with a solid four carat sparkler on her finger. She didn't wear a watch to an event.

Her dress was a one-off by Maria Grachvogel. Tight fitting and seductive, it managed to make Bettenfroid's aged body attractive. Combined with the jewellery, one might say she was over the top, but that was her personality. In fashion and in life, she wished to make a statement. She was at the top of the pyramid and she set the tone of the evening and the future. *Why not be over the top?* She thought. *If not her, then who?*

No one had ever worn the design before, nor would they in the future. Each of her dresses was itemised, preserved, and stored in preparation for her grand gesture upon her death whereby the Musée Galliera of

Paris would receive the entire collection as a representation of art and fashion over the previous half century. There, she would be immortalised alongside the likes of Marie-Antoinette.

Tonight was a relatively minor event. Thankfully, no presidents or exalted company—their security was such a bore. Just billionaires, mere millionaires, and the politicians who wanted her to play match maker.

Her necklace felt odd as she walked down the sweeping stairs. All eyes were on her so she daren't adjust it, but something was definitely different. She shouldn't even be feeling anything but the weight against her bosom of the large stone. It felt as though the necklace was penetrating her skin, poisoning her blood and making her dizzy.

She tripped and fell from half way down the stairs. There was a collective gasp, undoubtedly from the politicians seeing their opportunity lost alongside the other guests' gasp of macabre fascination and possibly a little fear. Death and confronting mortality was always both fascinating and fear inspiring.

Amidst the cries of surprise came the shout, "call the paramedics! Is there a doctor in the house?"

A young woman stepped forward, immaculate in a simple black dress, with a row of studded diamonds in white gold around her neck. She didn't wear a watch either. "I am," she said. "Make some room. Don't touch her."

The crowd parted slightly and the young woman stepped forward, confident and poised. She kneeled the best she could in her dress. She had kicked off her heels and inched her dress up to allow her free movement. Madame Bettenfroid was a mangled mess at the bottom of the stairs. She didn't appear to be breathing.

The doctor gently repositioned her so she could administer CPR prior to the medics arriving. People jostled to get clear but also to stay near. This was the best show in town and would be talked about for decades—everyone knew the power of saying "I was there" when the conversation would drift to this event.

The doctor prepared the air waves and began depressing Bettenfroid's chest. Broken bones and other injuries would need to wait. She had to start the heart and lungs. The doctor's glossy black hair hung over Bettenfroid like a cowl. It shook and bobbed as the doctor alternated between chest and mouth in a fury of activity. No one could tell that she was simply ensuring her kill remained dead.

∞

British Columbia, Canada

Mr. Clark was hunting big game in the Rocky Mountains four hours by helicopter from Prince George, British Columbia, Canada. He had a ticket to hunt a grizzly bear. Male only. He never ate the meat, thinking it too gamey for his pallet, but he loved the helicopter ride and the crew he shot with. Today he was hunting with the vice president of the United States.

The plan was to fly into the middle of one of BC's great expanses of government-owned land, where the rangers had indicated an over population of bears. Carter wanted to shoot one with a compound bow but the secret service refused to let the VP be put in that type of danger. To kill a bear with a bow meant shooting within sixty yards of the beast. That is very close when a miss probably meant death. Naturally, Carter would have a .50 calibre handgun on him just in case. He told himself he would empty all of the magazine into the bear if that happened. Then he would need to change his underwear. He didn't argue with the suggestion to stick with high calibre rifles only.

The first day saw nothing but deer and the smaller mountain dwellers. Carter enjoyed the peace and power of letting those helpless creatures live. The weather was unbearable on the second day. Carter emailed his friends: "Un-bear-able to hunt today!"

The third day was good, with little to no wind, sunshine, and enough cloud to ensure the temperature didn't drop too low. It really wasn't much fun to hunt when the temperatures dropped below minus 10.

He dowsed himself in fox urine and other sprays and ointments his local sports store pushed on him. The VP did the same.

To be safe, both Carter and the VP took up position in separate trees and waited. That's all they could do. The bear was smarter, faster, and stronger than them. They had a gun. The bear would never come within a hundred yards of them except by accident if they were walking. Safety and common sense dictated positions in trees. Armed with .308s, a flask of coffee, and some sandwiches, they waited for their prey to come to them.

While they waited, pretending to hunt bear, a real hunter stalked them. They were easy targets. Loud and brash, they were stationary targets for hours on end.

Rodriguez maintained a distance of a thousand yards until she saw them settle into their positions. Approaching them from their blind sides, she made her way to within 350 yards. She could see them both. Her target was simple but it would be hard to cover this up. She could only take one shot or her position would be given away and the remaining crew would come hunting her. She fancied her chances but the smart move was to do the job and get out. No complications.

She put herself into position and targeted Clark. His head was as clear as an IMAX image. She just needed to determine where to shoot. When she did, the noise was deafening and the forest erupted with birds and little animals.

What happened next was a bit of good luck for Rodriguez. She had decided after much agonising not to use the sound suppressor. The VP was so wound up in anticipation of a grizzly that he fired his rifle upon hearing Rodriquez's shot, not realizing it wasn't fired by Carter. He fired off only one shot. The secret service checked in via radio to hear a babbling, incoherent VP. They were there in double time. They found the body of Carter, which had fallen from his tree, with a gunshot wound to the head. The VP was crying. He thought his shot killed Carter.

The secret service seemed to have a contingency plan for this. While the VP knew he had just shot the golden goose who would make him president, the agents took Carter's gun and pointed it at his head. They pulled the trigger.

"Mr. Vice President, we need to report this terrible accident," said the lead agent. "I really don't know how Mr. Carter did it but he managed to shoot himself in the head." The agent looked directly at the VP. "Isn't that so, Mr. Vice President?"

The future president was shaking but collected his senses. "Why, it was the darndest thing. He was getting a cup of coffee and the sling slipped. I guess he accidently pulled the trigger and it was all over."

The silence was complete. The agents did their job to protect the VP and his office. The VP survived an impossible situation, and Rodriguez didn't have to worry about a cover up. It would be done for her. She made a note to document what happened and sell the info to her boss—or just keep it for insurance.

Chapter Thirteen

A Proposal

After his meeting with Jack in London, Wang Wei informed his boss of his findings. He was instructed to create a dossier on those responsible. He was then to smash this order and expose them for who and what they were, just as the Bavarian prince did to the Illuminati all those years ago.

With help from Jack, Wei compiled eleven names who would shortly pay for their actions. But Wei also saw an opportunity one gets once in a lifetime. After much deliberation, he decided to act on his hunch. It would either get him killed or elevated to the top echelons of global power.

Reading Jack's dossiers, he soon realised that the key decision makers were Roth and Rock. They would never meet with such a lowly party functionate as himself without a good reason. He also realised that they needed to invite him. To that end, he prepared a truncated file to be delivered to Mr. Rock. All Wei needed to do was wait.

∞

"We have a situation," Mr. Rock said to the seated figure in the adjoining chair. The two had convened an emergency meeting. Ostensibly, they were visiting guests of dignitaries gathered in Montreux, Switzerland. The gathering was to discuss the most recent crisis facing the global economy, especially China's new role as a fully-fledged participant at the "adult table" as some called it. The IMF had re-jigged its basket of currencies within the SDR as of 2016 to reduce the US dollar to just over 41%, the euro at just under 31%, and China's yuan at just under 11%. The UK's pound sterling was at 8% and Japan's yen at just over 8%. Now the IMF wanted China to engage more fully with the world. One aspect of this meant free-floating currency values. Ironically, this would herald the yuan into a de facto reserve currency. The world debated the consequences with most participants blissfully unaware that this was the desire of the Order of the Prime and many of the debates had been framed by them. The order had learned long ago that one of the best tools in the world of transparency and debate is the power of setting the question to be answered.

"Perhaps you are over-reacting?" Roth said. He was the other party in the adjoining chair. The two were the engines of the prime. At times they despaired of whether and when they would find a successor to their life's work.

"Not this time. I received a message. It was discreet but it left no doubt that we must meet and that the stakes are very high." Rock didn't like to be summoned, but he was a pragmatist first and foremost. He had decided to meet, with or without Roth.

Roth had known Rock for nearly six decades. He had never seen him cave in to pressure. He trusted Rock and knew that his fate was intertwined with his own. He too was a pragmatist.

"It's a shame about the timing," Roth said. "A century of work, four decades of which was ours. Our patience during the dollar experiment culminated in the precursor to our goal of a single global currency and the end of war as we know it." He was referring to the now inevitable course China was inching towards in making its currency a global reserve. It would rise and fall and the inevitable crisis would herald the SDR or a branded equivalent onto the world stage.

Rock chuckled. "The Chinese have been treating the dollar for what it is: an anchor, a replacement for gold. In doing so, the distortion of the reality of the two economies' health created trade imbalances and cries of foul play by the West. In calling for the Chinese to float its currency, the seeds of a multiple reserve currency world were sown. Now we just need to sit back and reap our harvest."

"Yes, but first we must deal with our more immediate threat," Roth continued.

The two looked into the fire in silence. Atop a mountain overlooking Lake Geneva, warm in their private residence behind triple glazed glass, the two contemplated their next step.

∞

When Wei arrived at Du Parc, the private residences where Roth and Rock were staying, he was forced to walk fifty metres beyond where his car was allowed to stop. He was accompanied by six security staff, two in front and behind with one on each side of him. *Security's tighter than when my boss met the* US *president*, he thought to himself. He was taken into a ground floor entrance and told to wait in a room with no windows. He didn't wait long as a doctor and two security officers came in shortly thereafter. They asked him to strip naked and he was subjected to a full body cavity search. Satisfied, they allowed him to dress and follow them into another room without windows. Again, he was told to strip naked and was subjected to a full body x-ray. Again, satisfied, they allowed him to dress and follow them into another room, this time with windows. He was offered tea and some sandwiches and an assortment of chocolates and cookies.

"Excuse me sir," Wei said. "Is this treatment usual to all of your employer's guests?" The process hadn't started just today. Three days ago, his passport was required to be physically handed over and was only returned after the x-rays today. He received calls from friends and colleagues about requests for information and odd phone calls. Obviously they were checking up on him.

"Nothing is usual about your visit, sir," came the reply.

"Do you know when I might be able to see them?"

"No. But the fact you are where you are is a good sign." The suited man left Wei alone.

"I guess one learns something every day," Wei said to himself. "At least the views are spectacular." The morning mist and fog had burned off with the cloudless sun. The mountains stood majestically above the lake, filling Wei's entire field of vision.

A door opened and two figures stepped inside. Their movement was slow and studied, more from the fear of falling than anything else. They were both in robust health for their ages but a broken hip from carelessness would still be an inconvenience neither could tolerate. Both were dressed in dark blue, pinstriped suits, crisp white shirts and polished black shoes. They both were immaculately groomed with skin that looked twenty years their junior. They exuded power, confidence and authority.

Wei stood immediately and approached them with hand extended. "Mr. Rock, Mr. Roth, it's a pleasure to meet you. My name is Wang Wei." The three men had firm handshakes. Wei was impeccably turned out in a tailored suit from Jermyn Street, London, and custom shoes from a firm in Vienna that once crafted shoes for the Hapsburgs. Wei enjoyed the finer things that life offered and indulged in the pleasures of the simple luxuries lost in the bustle of modern life. He considered therapeutic baths in salts or sulphur an essential part of living, along with ayurvedic oiled massages. His native land provided him with the techniques of meditation and he was a repeat patient of the worlds' best acupuncturists. His goal was to restrict his medicines to those grown from the earth, but he wasn't so foolish as to dismiss the miracles of modern technology and medicine. The latter he reserved for mechanical functions or ailments like heart attacks or joint replacements. In like manner, his meeting with Rock and Roth was to be either holistic or surgical. If holistic, he could do a deal. If surgical, the only result would be to cut the cancer out. *If he survived this visit,* he thought to himself.

"You have us at a disadvantage, Mr. Wang," started Roth.

"Please, call me Wei," he said. "But I doubt there is anything I know that you don't already." He smiled deferentially.

"I'm not so sure about that," Rock said. He also managed a thin smile. He was impressed with Wei.

"Can we offer you a drink?" Roth said. He nodded towards the fully stocked bar.

"No, thank you," Wei said. "I believe you have some questions of me."

"Yes, of course. Please sit down." The three of them sat in front of the fireplace. Lake Geneva was silent in the distance below.

"You are probably wondering why I asked to meet you both," Wei started.

Both men nodded slightly. It was a nonsense as all three parties knew exactly what was to be discussed. But it was a nonsense which was to be respected as none of the parties knew how this was going to end.

"It has come to my attention that a secret order has been operating for some time, contrary to the interests of China and my boss, the general secretary."

Wei paused. Rock and Roth looked straight at him, their breathing imperceptible. Perhaps they even were holding their breath. Despite himself, Rock was enjoying feeling alive—a little fear and the unknown were rare emotions to him and had been for quite some time.

"I have been instructed to identify this order, smash it into non-existence, and make known any and all of its secrets."

Rock and Roth lifted their chins slightly. This nobody was threatening them in their own home. But they weren't looking at a nobody in their minds; they were looking at China and wanted to know how much Wei's superiors knew.

"But I have learned quite a lot in my investigations of your group," Wei continued. "In fact, I have grown fond of your underlying philosophy."

Rock and Roth exhaled. They had contingencies in place. Wei could disappear and all questions would be hushed. But the greatest prizes weren't won by not taking chances. Wei was an opportunity for them. They were waiting to see how he would play his hand.

"My concern," Wei said, "is that you are not allowing China to become who she might be. Your goals are to create the impossible. A world without war through a single currency and, ultimately, a single arbiter of legal disputes and financial settlements."

It was Roth's turn to speak. "Our goal is simple and precise. The global institutions were put in place to provide a forum where nations could exchange words instead of gunfire. While we support those institutions, we don't control them. How could we?"

It was Wei's turn to smile. "That is what makes your order so attractive to me. It is the shear impossibility of your control that makes its existence hard for me to destroy. It is like a rare species, delicate and extremely dangerous. Make no mistake, it's not difficult to destroy; it is just outside of my ability. I have come to admire it a little too much."

What Rock wanted to say was, *"Who are you to say that you could crush it? Something that has survived two centuries would not feel the dent of your greatest exertions. You may think you know what we are and what we do and what our weaknesses are. But you don't have a clue. You are not the only one with an army at your back."* Instead, he opted to say, "Perhaps

I speak for both of us," Rock said, "but what do you want to do? You have, as a gambler might say, all the cards."

"I have a proposal for you. It's simple and straight forward. I need to seek revenge for your actions, as I was assigned by my boss, but I also want to join your order, as an equal, to ensure the continued success of China. I will need your help. China will need your help. Eventually, the world will need our help."

Rock barely suppressed a laugh. "That's all? And what do you bring to the table?"

Wei ignored the laugh. It was Rock's prerogative. "I can bring to the table that which you yearn for: China's integration into your economic system."

It was Roth who then said, "But how can you deliver this. China's internal workings are legendary for their intricacy. No one man can deliver this, least of all you. I expected more from you Mr. Wang."

"Then let me prove myself. I will give you a copy of everything I have on you and your order of Prime. That's a gift. I will submit the other's names as justice must be meted out. I will do everything you ask of me with the understanding that if I deliver and China comes on board, you will allow me to join." Wei paused and then added, "besides, you will need to rebuild a successor to your existing order. And I am the type of person you want on your team."

"Mr. Wang, that is an interesting proposal. I will need to discuss this with Mr. Rock and get back to you. In the interim, you will be our guest."

The three got up and shook each other's hands. They each looked at the other fully in the face as they did so. *I do like this kid*, thought both Rock and Roth to themselves. *Finally, someone with balls.*

∞

Within three months of Wei's meeting with Rock and Roth, the general secretary agreed to float the yuan at a time to be determined by his advisors. The yuan would join the dollar and the euro as global reserve currencies, alongside the British pound and the Japanese yen. The stage was now set. It was just a matter of time before the envisioned crisis took place. It didn't matter whether it was two or twenty two years, or longer. The foundation was solid.

∞

When Mary Rodriguez eventually received her version of the dossier with eleven names marked for death, it was through the usual channels. Rodriguez would think she was being instructed by the CIA or some other US government agency. She may have been an assassin, but she was no traitor.

Chapter Fourteen

Changing of the Guard

Jack read the news of the deaths of Bettenfroid and Carter. Those were hard for the press to suppress. Carter was a scandal due to the proximity of his death and the vice president. It was spun as a near miss to the VP and policy was being discussed to include psychological evaluations on anyone who could get close to the president or vice president. It was unlikely to gain traction but the media enjoyed their talking heads.

What he didn't read was the murder of Franca, Oberdorff, and the five other members of the order. He didn't hear about Clog's death until his new handler made contact. The CIA had decided to let Jack go into sleeper mode and would be in touch in due course.

Jack didn't know how to react when he heard the news. He was elated and fearful in equal measure. If they could get to Clog, how would he survive?

The news continued with the story of the Chinese general secretary's ill health. Two weeks later, he died peacefully in his sleep. Three days of mourning was declared. Jack recognised the Chinese fellow he met in London in some of the photos, always off to the side.

Jack's parents had made contact with G29. After Clog's assassination, it was deemed safe for them to return. He was having dinner with them tonight.

Carey never returned from the UK. Jack took this badly and was barely able to function for weeks, but that too passed. He wondered at the resilience of the human spirit. While his heartbreak was not in the same category as war, famine, disease, and extreme poverty, he could see how the body absorbs shock, pain, and terror and normalises the experience. Once something becomes normal, life goes on. It recalibrates and overcomes.

He opened a bottle of Italian red wine to go with his venison stew. He used prunes to provide a textured sweetness to the stew and ensured that enough carrots and potatoes were there. The meat was given to him by a friend and he put balsamic vinegar, garlic, and onions on it and let it sit all day in the slow cooker. He was proud of his stew. Simple and tasty.

When his parents arrived, the three of them felt a relief they hadn't enjoyed for years. They had made it and survived the biggest test of their lives. They were all alive, the correct authorities were made aware of the secretive order, and the CIA agent Clog was no longer.

Jack felt a wince of guilt over Clog. He had included Clog's name on the list given to Wei. That was part of the plan his parents outlined to him when they reappeared in his life shortly after his graduation. The double double cross.

There was a knock on the door and all three heads swivelled in unison.

"You expecting anyone, Jack?" James said.

"No. Let me just check who it is." Jack got up and went to the door. He looked through and relaxed, calling back to his parents, "It's only Joe."

Jack opened the door.

"Hi Jack," Joe said. He was getting old and his movements were increasingly slow.

"Hi Joe. What's up?"

"I noticed your lights were on and thought I'd drop by. I hope you don't mind."

The house didn't sell so they were having dinner there. James and Denise were wary of cities and preferred to stay on the move. This was their first time back to the family home since that night Jack waited for them to have ice cream and discuss their plan. That was the night James and Denise ran. It seemed like a lifetime ago. Two lifetimes.

"Come on in, Joe," James said. He had got up and pulled out a chair for Joe before walking towards him and holding out his hand. They shook and hugged. "Good to see you looking so well."

"Thanks. You two also look remarkably well, considering," Joe said. He went around the table to give Denise the customary two pecks on the cheeks and then a proper hug. Just before he sat down he handed Jack a bottle of 1955 Chateau Lafite. "You may want to open this and let it breathe a bit before pouring."

Jack looked at the bottle and his eyes weren't sure if he saw correctly. "1955? Joe, maybe this is a mistake? This must have cost a fortune. Besides, it'll be wasted on me. I don't know enough about wine to deserve this."

"Nonsense. If you don't drink it, how will you learn? Maybe you already know and just need some guidance? Besides, if I can't share this with the three people I love the most, who shall I share it with? And when? I'm not getting any younger." With that, Joe smiled and enjoyed the adulation of his friends. Each one made a point to say how extravagant the gesture was.

The four of them sat down and began to eat Jack's stew. He became conscious that he should have made more of an effort to make something nice for the event, but his wine and stew went down well. The conversation flowed easily and was punctuated with laughter and genuine love from one person to the next. When the food was eaten and the first bottle gone, Jack brought out Joe's bottle and put it on the table reverently. He rummaged in the fridge and found some cheeses. As he served the cheese, he wished he had thought of taking it out of the fridge before the meal started. During his crash course on etiquette in London, he learned that cheese increasingly was served as the French enjoy it—at room temperature. In that manner, it can be tasted and the flavours come forward. As he couldn't turn back time, he found some biscuits to go with the cheese and placed them the best he could on the table.

He pulled out the best red wine glasses and he deposited enough to fill the bottom fifth of the glass, careful to not pour too much. They all waited for their glasses to be filled before declaring the customary toasts full of love and health and happiness. Joe's eyes were filling up by the time the speeches ended.

When the last of the cheese and wine were finished, they retired to the lounge and fell into their favourite chairs. Jack took the sofa and sprawled himself across like he was still fourteen.

"Did you ever wonder at the odds of us all being in the same town together at the same time in history?" Joe asked no one in particular.

"History? That may be getting a little bit grand for our pay scale," James started, "but time, yes. It was remarkable that we could find a person of your intelligence, background, and..."

His voice stopped midsentence and Jack turned to look at him. He saw his father with blood pouring down his neck onto his chest, with his hands clasped to his throat. His mother's eyes opened wide and she turned to look at Joe. Just then her head snapped back as the bullet tore into the side of her nose, just under the eye, causing the wall behind her to be splattered with blood and bits of brain. She didn't make a sound after that. James was gurgling and looked towards Joe when the next bullet hit his front teeth, shattering the years of brushing and flossing, and continued through the roof of his mouth and out the back of his head. His blood was all over his favourite chair. The brain matter couldn't be distinguished from the existing pattern on the chair.

Jack watched in horror and disbelief. It was fast and slow at the same time. The brain must have watched it in normal time but then re-wound and watched it again and again, catching more detail of the scenes playing out in front of Jack.

When the sound of the .45 ceased and all that re-mained in the room was death, Joe turned slowly to Jack. "I loved them so." Tears were streaming down his face.

Still too stunned to talk or react, Jack looked at Joe with an expression of heartbreak, fear, and betrayal. Anger would come later, if there was a later. His eye-lids opened and closed rapidly. He couldn't stop them. His body started to shake with spasms starting from his neck to his knees. His fingers were moving and head bobbled. The shock was causing his body to shut down.

"Son, I had no choice." The tears were free flowing down the old man's face. The stubble of facial hair held the salty water back from falling directly from his chin. "James and Denise, your parents, they made their choice." His voice broke. "They knew how this would end. The way it had to end."

Jack continued to shake. He thought about rushing Joe but realised he was out of his league. He found his voice. "Why Joe? Why? What did they ever do to you?" It came out quiet, like a whisper. But his mind was yelling it at the top of his lungs.

"Nothing. That's why this is so cruel and unfair. Unfair to them, unfair to you, and unfair to me. They should never have told me to do this!"

"They?" Jack was trying to stand, his legs shaky. He was backing away from Joe. Tears were running freely down his cheeks but he felt nothing.

Joe stopped crying, aware he had let his mask slip. His guard was down and Jack was one of the few who he would allow to see behind the facade. But he still was who he was and he hadn't lived as long as he had by being careless.

"You don't want to know, Jack."

Jack found his voice and screamed, "You just fucking killed my parents in front of me. You fucking owe me this, Joe." Jack had backed up to the lounge's entrance. He wanted to run but his legs could still barely keep him upright.

Joe pursed his lips. "Your parents were part of an ultra-secret department of the CIA called Group 29.

This whole mess that you got involved in was as a result of their actions within the G29."

"Who the fuck cares!?" screamed Jack. He felt dinner rising in his throat as he glimpsed the dead corpses that once were his parents. "Why'd you kill my parents?" He started breaking down, the tears turning into sobs.

"I'm also part of G29. I was recruited in Korea and retired to this town. When your parents were relocated here, it wasn't by accident. It was so that I could keep an eye on them. I was retired, but as you now know, you can never retire and never escape. Death is their final parting gift. If I didn't do it, someone else would have, and it would not have been so clean, so pleasant. Think torture of the worst form and then multiply it be a hundred. You really don't want to know. I wish I didn't." Joe stopped talking and his face turned grey. "That's why I decided to take this assignment."

Jack couldn't handle any more talk. His dinner was on the floor, his clothes soaked with sweat and everything he believed in was over. He slumped to the floor, back to the wall, unable to stand any longer. "So you just need to kill me and then live happily ever after?" His voice was defiant. His body was sore from the shaking and shock.

"I don't want to kill you, Jack. These hands held you as a little boy, picked you up as a child, and applauded you as a man."

"If you're not going to kill me, what are you going to do?"

"I'm going to give you a chance to live. I'll need to explain myself and deal with the consequences, but I want you to live. More than you could ever know."

Jack wasn't expecting that. "But I can't run from people like this. They know all and see all."

Joe snorted. "They don't know or see as much as you think."

"But you just said you can never retire and never escape. What makes you think that I can run and survive? Wouldn't it just be better to kill me now?"

Joe nodded as if having a conversation with himself. It was a couple of seconds before he spoke. "You have to believe in something. Why not yourself?"

"I'm not interested in your pep talk, Joe. You are permanently in my shit book. You may as well just kill me now." Jack was resigned, like a bunny in a dog's mouth, not dead but knowing full well what was going to happen. The mouth just needed to close. Jack waited.

"Life is easier when your enemy is identified and defined. You are fortunate enough to know who your enemy is. You don't need to waste time on ghosts or fantasies. Your enemy is very real and very powerful, but you can survive. Stay low, stay invisible. Stay alive."

"Why are you telling me this? Why are you helping me?"

"That I won't tell you. Now get the hell out of here before I change my mind."

Jack kept his back to the wall and inched along the perimeter until he got near the front door. He backed out and then sprinted into the night air. He was on the run and would be the rest of his life.

Back in the house, Joe looked at Denise and James. It was a dirty business, this. He caressed Denise's face and looked at the pictures of Jack on the wall. He moved the bodies so that he could sit on the chair between them. He looked at Denise one last time. Then at James. Then he pulled the trigger.

Chapter Fifteen

The Road Taken

Jack heard the final shot as Joe joined his parents in the great silence that is death. He only had the shirt on his back and a few dollars in his pocket. He was in the middle of nowhere with knowledge of a global conspiracy and targeted for death by the ultra-secret G29 of the CIA.

His prospects didn't look great.

But he was alive and he intended to stay alive.

As he ran down his childhood street, he passed Joe's house. The lights were off and there was an old blue and silver Ford F150 pickup truck in the driveway. He had never seen the truck there before. Something inside him caused him to slow down and look at the old Ford. Another part of him screamed to fun faster.

Jack looked at the old truck. There was some rust but not too bad considering its age. It wasn't a total beater. It must have been from the eighties. He tried the door and it opened. Inside he found a note, a folded piece of paper, with his name on it.

Dear Jack,

If you are reading this, then things have gone according to plan. I don't blame you if you hate me for the rest of your life. I deserve that. But now your parents and I are dead and you need to stay alive. You know what you are up against. You know the challenges ahead. As a parting gift, I want you to have this truck. Use it contents wisely. There is food and camping supplies in the back. There is a rifle and a handgun with plenty of ammunition. Both guns are untraceable.

There is cash as well as gold hidden in the truck so please don't lose it or have it stolen until you have made these items safe. I have left you some instructions separately and I bequeath you all my earthly possessions.

Be quick and go. Don't speed. Remember that fast is slow and slow is fast in your circumstances. Be certain before you act. But act you must.

I loved you like my own son,

Yours,

Joe.

Jack held the paper without emotion. The shock was too great. All he knew was that he needed to survive long enough to disappear. He needed to get off the grid. Joe had proven himself to be the biggest sonofabitch, but Jack had loved him too. He was like a father, a mentor, and a friend.

After only a few more moments of stunned reflection, he settled himself behind the steering wheel. The keys were already in the ignition.

He inhaled deeply and exhaled, and then he turned the key.

An Invitation

The bar room table between us was littered with glasses, mugs, and snacks. Outside, the wind continued to howl and the sun had set hours ago. Other stranded travellers had come and gone and would likely return for an evening of drinking, but for the most part, we had been alone. We were alone when he finished his story.

"That was twenty years ago," Jack said.

"That's one hell of a story," I said. I rarely interrupted him except to order food or drink or visit the men's room.

"It was a scary time," he said.

"Why me? After all this time, why let me in on your secret?"

"Most of what I told you has already come to pass and the key players are all dead. I just needed to tell it. I can't explain it better than that. It's like an itch that has been gathering inside me. I'm not a religious man but I've been told that confession is good for the soul. Not just for absolution, but for the act of letting it go."

"Do you feel better?"

"Strangely, yes. I've been on the run so long it has become second nature to me."

"And the authorities?"

"They're not looking for me anymore. In many ways, there's no reason for me to be on the run. I've dropped off the grid and stayed there. I figured out how to manage funds without tripping any red flags. I have a network of people I can rely on when I need to."

"How did you find those people? How do you know you can trust them?"

"I have a good feeling about these things. If I feel comfortable, I tell them my story."

"And in return," I said, "they tell you theirs?"

"Something like that."

"And then what happens?" I asked.

"We shake hands and if we can help each other we do."

I was silent. It was an invitation. I'd never offered any explanation as to how I got here and he never asked. The storm was still blowing. We were still stuck.

"Maybe we should have a drink," I said.

"Sounds like a good idea," he said. "Scotch?"

"Beer please," I said.

We got our drinks, ordered some burgers and fries, and I told Jack why I was heading to Churchill.

ABOUT THE AUTHOR

Baron was born in Canada.
He currently lives in South East England,
somewhere near the Surry/Sussex borders.
Sightings vary.

If you'd like to follow Baron and receive free samples
of his future writing before it is published, please visit
www.baronalexanderbooks.com